A Candlelight Ecstasy Romance®

"THIS IS ONE TIME DADDY'S MONEY ISN'T GOING TO BUY YOU SOMETHING, LADY!"

Harper's mouth twisted with the anger inside him. "I'll have this hotel. You'll lose."

"Oh, that's very doubtful. Remember, you should never underestimate the competition."

"Hey, Alexis, I like competition. Real competition, that is. I don't see you as much of a serious threat."

"We'll see about that. I doubt you'll be acting quite so arrogantly when we're all through here. I'm the one who's going to own the Ebbtide."

"Over my dead body!" He studied Alexis for a second longer. "If you think for one minute that I'm going to roll over and play dead simply because a woman I'm attracted to wants the same thing I do, you're very naive. I didn't get where I am playing kids' games."

Alexis's eyes smoldered with fire as she brought her face even closer to his. "Neither did I, but don't worry about it. The attraction was entirely imaginary."

CANDLELIGHT ECSTASY ROMANCES®

LAUGHTER'S WAY

Paula Hamilton

A CANDLELIGHT ECSTASY ROMANCE®

Published by
Dell Publishing Co., Inc.
1 Dag Hammarskjold Plaza
New York, New York 10017

ISBN: 0-440-14712-3

Printed in the United States of America
First printing—January 1985

This book is dedicated
to
Kim and Paige
Light of my life

To Our Readers:

We have been delighted with your enthusiastic response to Candlelight Ecstasy Romances®, and we thank you for the interest you have shown in this exciting series.

In the upcoming months we will continue to present the distinctive, sensuous love stories you have come to expect only from Ecstasy. We look forward to bringing you many more books from your favorite authors and also the very finest work from new authors of contemporary romantic fiction.

As always, we are striving to present the unique, absorbing love stories that you enjoy most—books that are more than ordinary romance. Your suggestions and comments are always welcome. Please write to us at the address below.

Sincerely,

The Editors
Candlelight Romances
1 Dag Hammarskjold Plaza
New York, New York 10017

CHAPTER ONE

"What the h—"

The elevator was plunged into sudden darkness and came to a jarring halt.

"Are you all right?"

Alexis Cartwright sighed softly. "Yes, I'm fine." Of all the luck, she thought. Stuck in a darkened hotel elevator when she was already late for her appointment—an extremely important appointment at that.

"The electricity must have gone off. It'll be back on in just a minute," a husky masculine voice echoed across the tiny enclosure.

Tiny creaking sounds became increasingly pronounced, streaming into her consciousness. The muted strains of scraping metal, unidentifiable popping noises; everything became magnified in the pitch-blackness as time dragged by.

"There's no need to worry. It probably won't be but another minute or two."

"I don't believe I'm the one who's worried," she replied, smiling into the darkness. She'd taken note of the rapid-fire way the man had spoken as well as the tenseness in his tone.

"Has this ever happened to you before?" the voice demanded.

"No, it hasn't." She was trying to remember what this talkative man looked like. He'd stepped into the hotel elevator at the same time she had, and they were all alone, but for the life of her she couldn't recall his face.

Concentration was impossible. It made her uncomfortable to talk to someone she couldn't see. There was something about being thrust into absolute darkness that made her feel a little strange, as if she wanted to touch herself all over to make sure she was still there.

"Well, I've been stuck in one of these things before." Harper Evans waited for a second, and when the woman didn't reply, he went on despite the hint of exasperation he'd earlier caught in her voice. "Be grateful there are only two of us in here and that our luggage was sent up ahead of us. Once I got stuck like this with an elevator full of men attending a law enforcement convention."

Not knowing exactly what was expected of her and wishing he wouldn't talk quite so much, she replied, "That must have been very uncomfortable, being so crowded and all."

"At first it was fun," Harper went on, rewarded by her polite response. He was determined to get her to talk to him. Spending an afternoon in an outmoded old elevator with a perfect stranger wasn't his idea of a good time, but he'd make the best of it. "When I finally got out of there, I was without my wallet. It seems I was with a group of men who'd come to tell the conventioneers how to stop crime in their neighborhoods. They were all reformed—or not quite so reformed—thieves."

When he'd finished his sentence, she could hear an infectious, low rumble of laughter. The preposterousness of the situation struck Alexis then and she joined in, laughing not so much at his joke as at the circumstances. "Well, then, since you seem to be the more experienced at this sort of thing, how long do you think we'll be stuck in here?"

"I'm not quite the expert I made myself out to be, so your guess is as good as mine." His words bounced back and forth along the metal walls. "If it doesn't come back on in a few minutes, though, it's going to get hotter than hell in here." He paused, noticing the rather dramatic temperature change already taking place. "Not much air circulates in old elevator shafts like this one."

Frantically, her mind raced, scrambling back to when she'd stepped inside the elevator. A frown creased her forehead as she tried to force herself to remember this man's face.

She vaguely remembered that he had been somewhat attractive, not dramatically so, but interesting-looking. Elevator etiquette being what it was, she hadn't looked directly at him, and now she couldn't recall any specifics, only that his suit had fit him well. Everything else was a total blur.

Tentatively, Alexis touched the paneled elevator wall with her fingertips. "If you had a match or a lighter we could try to find the emergency button. Maybe that would help."

From across the way she heard a rustling noise, and then the man's footsteps lightly resounded in the quiet space. The musky scent of his aftershave wafted toward her, jarring her senses. In the inky black darkness she could barely keep her sense of direction, and she abruptly turned to move out of his way.

"I don't think it will do any good, but I'll try it. Lucky for us I just happen to have a lighter. I carry it around from force of habit. I quit smoking a while ago."

His husky voice was startling; so near she could feel it in the air around her. All at once she felt something bump up against her left shoulder, and then she was being roughly shoved up against the elevator wall. "Oh . . ." she gasped as she fell. She felt a powerful arm wrap itself around her back; then it was brusquely pulling her up.

Every nerve in her body was awakened, alerted, and overloaded. For a few seconds she didn't know what had happened, couldn't identify what it was that had fallen heavily against her.

"Hey," the deep voice whispered in her ear, registering surprise of its own.

It was him. He had run into her when he'd stepped toward the control panel. It was his hard body she'd felt pressed against her own. She pushed frantically against his chest, trying to right herself.

A tiny feeling of fear washed over her. She didn't know this man at all. He could be anything or anyone, and here she was trapped in this darkened space with him. Had he clung to her just a little too long? she wondered. In slow motion she reached down for her purse, thought better of it, and instead grabbed her high-heeled shoe, her mind reeling with the possibilities of what he might try to do.

"Sorry about that. I can't see a damned thing in

here," he said, and reached out for the control panel while trying to flick his lighter on.

She felt an arm glance against her breast, and then she heard an unidentifiable clicking sound. Without a moment's hesitation she swung the heel of her shoe up and over with all her might, and when she made contact she brought her arm back behind her, ready to swing again.

"My God," he yelled, not certain what was happening. "What in the hell is that?" Harper flicked on the cigarette lighter and reached out in time to catch her arm with his other hand.

For a brief second their eyes met, but before their eyes could adjust to the light, they were plunged back into darkness again. "Are you some kind of crazy or what?" he asked, full of indignation. "Look, it was an accident. I'm going over to my own corner now. Okay?"

He remembered how her pale blue eyes had been rounded in fear. There was no telling what this woman might try to do. Listening for any unusual noises coming from behind him, he cautiously stepped away from her, still wondering what she had attacked him with.

More to himself than to her, he said, "Anybody who wants that damned emergency button pushed can push it without any more help from me. This good samaritan is retiring right here and now." He rubbed the top of his head, fully expecting to find a warm gush of blood there.

Remaining alert, still gripping her shoe in one hand, Alexis felt for the wall, found the control panel, and shakily but methodically began to press

13

every button she could find. Nothing worked, but she doggedly persisted. It gave her something to do with herself while she struggled to calm down. Maybe she'd made a mistake.

"You ought to be ashamed of yourself. At least you ought to try apologizing," the voice insisted, but Alexis remained quiet. She was still breathing hard.

"Don't you have anything at all to say for yourself?" the stranger persevered.

Still wound too taut from her ordeal, she leaned her head back against the wall, thwarted by her situation and the asinine way she was handling herself.

"How could I have gotten so lucky?"

She heard the futility in the voice from across the way. Obviously, he was as frustrated as she, but conversation didn't interest her right now.

The minutes seemed like hours, and Alexis looked down at her gold watch, wishing she could see what time it was. By now she knew she'd missed her appointment with Sally Ferguson, the aging owner of the Ebbtide Hotel, but surely the woman would understand. More than likely, the entire ten floors were without electricity.

If Alexis was able to purchase the hotel, she made a vow to herself that the first thing she'd do would be to have the entire structure inspected carefully, beginning with the electrical wiring and the elevator. She heard a ponderous thumping from somewhere above them, and she twisted her head to look up, knowing full well she'd see only blackness.

"Hey, down there. Is anybody there?" someone shouted from above them.

"Yes," she heard her companion call out. "There are two of us in here."

"Okay, listen. We're going to have the electricity back on shortly, but just in case we don't get everything working within the next hour, we'll climb down and get you."

"Great, just great," the now familiar raw-edged voice answered. She heard him mumble loudly, "I'm stuck with a maniac down here and you tell me it could be another hour!"

Her own frustration increasing by the second, Alexis decided not to let his presumptuous insinuation pass. "I'm not the maniac in this elevator," she called out in the darkness.

"Oh, no? Then tell me what sort of sane woman would attack a fellow who was trying to help her out."

"Is that what you call it?"

"Oh, Lord, help me out of here!" he exclaimed. "Of course that's what I call it. How could you think it was anything else?"

The way he presented his case made her feel a little foolish. "Well, I'll admit that perhaps I misjudged you," she ventured, wishing she could see him when she talked. "But think about it from my vantage point. I'm stranded here like this. I have no way of getting out. I can't see a thing, and suddenly I'm knocked down by some stranger."

"Do you know my ex-wife?" he interrupted her.

"What?"

"My ex-wife. Her name's Helena. Helena Evans."

"No," she gasped. "Of course not."

"I think you two probably met someplace, and she

hired you to come and irritate me like this, didn't she?"

"Don't be ridiculous," Alexis replied, certain now that if he wasn't any of the awful things she'd supposed, he was at least a little unusual.

"Evidently, you don't know my ex-wife, then, or you'd know nothing is ridiculous where she's concerned. . . ." His voice trailed off with a hint of humor.

Despite everything she'd been through, everything she'd been feeling, she had to laugh. The man had a finely honed wit about him. Suddenly, she found herself curious about this stranger and his relationship with his ex-wife. She felt like some comment was in order. "Life isn't always a bed of roses, is it?"

"Hardly," he replied.

The heat was becoming intolerable, and Alexis reached up to take off her linen suit jacket and, with a flick of her wrist, adjusted her silk blouse. If she was going to have to remain there much longer, she should at least be as comfortable as possible. Carefully, she folded the jacket before draping it across her arm.

"What are you doing? I can hear you. Don't come any closer!" the man joked.

"I'm not the one who stumbles over people. Remember?" she admonished him. Once more, she listened to the sounds in the elevator, but there was nothing.

"That was the most honest of accidents, really. The same thing could have happened to you." Responding to the stale, hot air, he began to remove his jacket. "It's hot in here. I'm going to sit down. From

16

the way it sounds, it may be a long time before we leave."

"Weren't you the man who said we'd probably be out in a minute?"

He nodded, then remembered she couldn't see him. "Yeah, well, I don't know why you believed me when I said that about our getting out of here in a minute when you so obviously didn't trust me ten minutes later."

"Touché." His comment reminded her of her appointment with Miss Sally Ferguson. "Do you have any idea what time it is?" she asked him.

"I can't see my watch, but I'd guess . . . wait a second."

"What else have I got to do?"

They both laughed then, and he flicked his lighter briefly over the crystal face of his watch. "It's close to two o'clock. By the way," he went on, "my name is Harper Evans."

"How do you do, Mr. Evans. My name is Alexis Cartwright."

He listened to the soft, melodic way she spoke. Her voice was smooth with a richly drawled Southern accent. Funny, he thought. Her voice doesn't go along with the aggressive way she'd behaved earlier. "I'm glad to know you," he replied, and then chuckled. "That's not true. My aching head says that's not true at all."

His laughter was light and pleasant, and it made her want to join in, full of relief to find he was becoming more than a mere voice. Somehow that knowledge took away the remainder of her fear. "I'm sorry. Really I am. I hope you understand."

17

"I'm trying," Harper rallied. "That's the best I can do right now." He slid his back down against the hard elevator wall and sat on the dusty, carpeted floor. "This is typical, you know."

"What's that?"

"This elevator going haywire, the electricity being out and all. It's typical of an antiquated building like this."

"Hmmm," she replied, unwilling to agree with him. Restoring old buildings was part of her business. She didn't believe it was typical at all.

"This thing needs to be torn down. I'll bet they have trouble like this once a month."

"What makes you think so?" Alexis probed. It would be to her advantage to find out what this stranger thought of the hotel. Even if she didn't agree with him, listening to his opinions might help her make her final decision as to how much she'd offer for the Ebbtide.

"Well, maybe you didn't notice it, but when I stepped into the elevator, I saw two wires dangling loose from the cable box. There's no excuse for poor maintenance, and if it's in a spot as important and as visible as the elevator, it's probably everywhere." He thought for a moment. "I'm not trying to spoil your vacation or anything. The Texas coast has the most underrated beaches in the country, and I'm sure you'll have a nice stay here."

"I'm sure I will." She made a mental note to check out the wires he was referring to. This man sounded more knowledgeable than she had first thought.

He listened to the self-assurance in her voice. He'd only caught a glimpse of her when he'd gotten his

18

lighter working, and her eyes had been the major feature he'd observed. She sounded good, though. A woman who was all soft and lovely, he imagined, but one with a little fire in her. He liked that part the best. He'd had enough of those females who used their femininity and not their brains. "How long are you staying in Galveston, Alexis?"

It was the first time he'd said her name, and she listened to the way his deep voice held it momentarily and then let go. "About a week. And you?"

"Me, too. I'm here on business. In fact, if we get out of here by three o'clock, I'll have just enough time to get ready for my afternoon appointment."

"What kind of business are you in?" She took off her other shoe and sat down on the floor, too. She couldn't begin to guess how long they'd been trapped inside the elevator, but she was anxious to be set free. The worst part of it all was the absolute darkness. There wasn't a hint of light anywhere.

"Construction, mostly. New construction. You're sitting down now, aren't you?" he added with measured interest.

"Yes." Her voice floated closer to him. "No wonder you took such careful notice of the elevator."

"Yeah, it gets to be second nature after a while," he acknowledged. "And you? What brings you to Galveston? Vacation?"

"I'm here on business also." She wasn't willing to divulge too much. One thing Miss Sally Ferguson had been adamant about was secrecy. She didn't want Alexis to tell anyone about the Ebbtide's being up for sale, and Alexis had honored her wish.

The fewer people involved, the better Alexis's prospects would be for buying the hotel, and from what she'd seen of it, she had already fallen in love. The acquisition of the Ebbtide Hotel would bring her total to five. Five hotels in six years wasn't bad at all, she thought, especially when they'd all been old hotels badly in need of repair. Now all of the first four were not only beautifully renovated but bringing in enough money to finally begin to repay her investment. It was a dream come true, especially after the first few lean years.

"When you see me again this week, remind me not to get back in this elevator," his voice came to her through the darkness. "I think I'll walk the six flights up to my room. Now, tell me a little bit about yourself. Maybe by the time we've traded life stories, this old crate will be moving again."

"Why don't you begin, Mr. Evans. I'm not quite the talker you are; besides, there's really nothing much to tell." What would she say? That she had an independent streak as wide as the Brazos River? That she'd worked so hard to stay outside her father's enormous shadow that she was afraid she might not be the compassionate woman she longed to be? He wouldn't find her tale very interesting.

"I won't accept that. Ladies first."

She wished she could see his face. Right now she had the same feeling she always did when she talked on the telephone. She never felt comfortable speaking to someone without being able to see him. Searching for something to tell him, she recounted a little bit about herself. "My full name is Alexis Bain Cartwright; I'm thirty-two years old and I come from Houston. How's that?"

"Okay, I guess, although I was hoping for something a little meatier myself. Are you an introvert, an extrovert, or what? Do you have a lot of friends or do you prefer to spend your time alone?" He enjoyed asking questions. It made him feel that he knew people a little bit better when he heard their replies, and Alexis Bain Cartwright's voice held a certain quality that fed his curiosity. He wanted to know her better, even if he couldn't see her.

"All of the above. Some days I'm one way and other days another. I sometimes think I'm a chameleon of sorts." Strange, but it was as if they were totally alone in some distant place, effectively sealed off, away from the rest of the world.

"Now that's an interesting statement if I ever heard one. I'd like to be able to see you when we talk."

She peered questioningly through the darkness, startled to hear her own thoughts spoken aloud. Was she just imagining that there was an added hint of intimacy in his voice? she wondered.

"Oh, well," she replied nervously. "Your imagination is probably better than the real thing."

"I don't know about that." He pondered her words for a moment. "You sound delicious—like a rich strawberry sundae." He started to say more when suddenly the elevator began to surge upward. "Hey, we're moving!" Excitedly, he jumped up. "Still no lights, though."

Alexis stood, then slid her shoes back onto her feet and ran her fingers through her short cap of curls, glad that their conversation was at an end. He was on the verge of embarrassing her, and she had to wonder if he was so forward with all the women he knew or only those he couldn't see. "At last," she said softly.

The elevator came to an abrupt stop, and the doors creaked slowly open. A worried-looking man helped them out of the elevator and introduced himself as the manager of the Ebbtide, all the while apologizing profusely and explaining how they'd had to use an emergency power supply in order to rescue them.

Relieved that the ordeal was at an end, Alexis paid scant attention to his explanations. Blinking her eyes in an attempt to adjust to the light, she tried to resist the urge to look at the man she'd been locked away with for the last forty-five minutes. But the urge became so overwhelmingly powerful that she turned and looked straight into his eyes.

Harper took one look at her and exclaimed, "You're the perfume lady. I knew I smelled it in the elevator."

"The what?" she asked, dumbfounded at his outburst. She watched twinkling brown eyes mischievously study her, and she took note of the shock of dark brown hair and the row of straight white teeth revealed by his broad smile.

"The perfume lady. I saw you this morning when you registered downstairs and you dropped your makeup case. I walked by just about the time you broke that bottle of perfume." He laughed, taking in every line and curve of her body. "Say, Alexis, you made that lobby smell like a florist shop in a matter of seconds."

"Yes—well . . ." she stammered, feeling her cheeks redden.

He kept talking, willing her to stay where she was.

From the moment he'd looked into those incredible pale blue eyes of hers and seen that headful of ginger-colored curls, Harper Evans knew he was hooked. His taste usually ran to buxom blonds, but that was before he'd seen Alexis Cartwright, he told himself. "I think I'm in love," he said aloud, knowing he was being ridiculous and not even caring.

Attempting to ignore his comment, Alexis extended her hand to shake his. She'd been wrong, she told herself. He was much more attractive than she'd first thought.

He straightened powerful shoulders and reached down to take her small hand in his, caressing it rather than shaking it. Looking up at him, she couldn't ignore the way he kept watching her, his look bordering on expectation.

As they stood there in the hallway, Alexis wondered why she was letting all this happen inside her. It wasn't as if she hadn't experienced things like this before with other men. But this time her reaction was different, somehow disturbing.

She could feel some strange energy between them, which she couldn't quite define. He was obviously charming and humorous, but there was something else, too; something that appealed to her very much.

She looked into his brown eyes, and they seemed to change color as he gazed back at her. The slow, sensual line of his lips started out friendly and innocent and then built to a suggestive curve that seemed able to hold her thoughts in suspension while she watched it develop. It wouldn't do for her to stand here with this man another minute, trying to blot out the kinds of thoughts that were building inside her head.

"Good-bye, Mr. Evans. Perhaps we'll see one another again. Maybe we'll meet on the stairs, since the elevators don't seem to be our best way of getting around." She pulled her hand from his and turned to walk away. "Oh," she said, looking back with an expression of regret. "I'm sorry about your head. I hope you'll forgive me."

He stood there, watching her walk away. If he had never seen her face he'd still know what kind of woman she was, he told himself. Even in that elegantly fitted suit, she moved in a spirited, self-assured way. The more he saw, the more he liked.

"Hey, Alexis," he called down the long hall, and waited for her to stop. When she did, he gave her a quick smile and a shrug of his broad shoulders. "Why don't we continue our conversation over dinner tonight? What do you say?"

She stood looking back down the dimly lit hallway for quite a while before she responded. All her instincts told her to say no, but she finally nodded her assent.

"Downstairs at seven," he said, grinning triumphantly. "Watch for the guy who'll have his head swathed in white bandages, and remember, only the two of us will know why."

Continuing on her way, Alexis laughed quietly to herself. She wasn't having dinner with Harper Evans because he'd been so kind. She was having dinner with him because of the way she'd felt when he'd taken her hand in his. And something told her she needed no other reason than that one.

As she walked away, she heard him whistling far down the hallway. Her pulse raced a little faster when she recognized the melody, a richly romantic old tune, one of her favorites.

CHAPTER TWO

When Alexis entered her room, all her reasons for wanting to restore historic old hotels came back to her with a rush. Unusually large with high ceilings, the room captured the essence of history. An antique brass-and-crystal chandelier was suspended in the middle of the room and illuminated the entire space, spreading light across the walnut four-poster bed with its lace bedspread and freshly fluffed pillows. Across the room was a sitting area where a rose-colored Chippendale sofa was flanked by two chintz wing chairs.

Everything about the room suggested an earlier time, and it was partly that sense of serenity and romance that made Alexis love her work. The prospect of renovating this hotel, a once elegant building constructed before the turn of the century, made her heart soar with exhilaration. If all went well it wouldn't be long before the deteriorating plumbing, crumbling facade, and dilapidated furnishings would all be replaced, and the Ebbtide would be as beautiful as it once had been.

She wandered slowly into the bathroom, taking careful stock of all she saw. It seemed more than likely that Sally Ferguson had tried to give her an

26

especially good room, and when Alexis saw the cracked, white tile floor, the peeling wallpaper behind the claw-footed tub and the tarnished brass shower fittings, she knew that there must be other rooms in far worse condition. But it didn't matter to her. If the price was right, all of this could be reworked into a Texas showpiece, and a profitable one at that. Alexis licked her lips unconsciously, already estimating how much it would cost to have the antique tile replaced in all the bathrooms.

Anxious to talk to Sally Ferguson as soon as possible, Alexis headed toward the telephone on the bedside table.

Her finger hovered over the dial while she looked for Miss Ferguson's number. "One, one, zero," she said when the operator answered.

"I'm sorry, Miss Ferguson's private line is busy," the pleasant voice said. "Could I have her return your call, or would you rather leave a message?"

"Please ask her to call Miss Cartwright in room 611," Alexis said.

"Thank you, Miss Cartwright. I'll see that she gets the message," the operator said, and disconnected the line.

Pleased with the woman's efficiency, Alexis replaced the receiver and walked to the towering bay window, which overlooked the sandy beaches of Galveston, Texas.

On impulse, Alexis pushed open the window and immediately was rewarded with a gust of warm wind that blew the salty smell of the gulf in with it. She promised herself if she became the owner of the Ebbtide, she'd keep an apartment in it for herself.

27

This beautiful, small old hotel would be her coup —the first Alexis Bain Cartwright hotel in Texas. Without fanfare or publicity, she'd bought two in Oklahoma, and after two years of hard work she'd purchased and renovated hotels in Arkansas, but she'd never attempted to buy one before in her home state, where she thought the publicity of her family name would have ruined everything for her.

Watching brightly colored sailboats glide across the water, she relaxed against the windowsill, absorbed by the view and her own memories. No one had bothered to imagine the Cartwright name being associated with the hotel business. Compared to the dazzling excitement of gold and silver, hotels seemed very tame.

And so she'd kept her privacy—for a while. And by doing so, she'd been able to create a business all her own, without anybody's support, without anyone's guidance. That was the thing she was proudest of: She'd accomplished it all by herself.

The insistent buzz of the telephone brought her back to the task at hand. "Hello," she answered on the fourth ring.

"Miss Cartwright, this is Sally Ferguson. I understand you've had a little bit of bad luck this afternoon. I'm so sorry you've had such a poor welcome to the Ebbtide. I do hope I can make it up to you." The woman's voice crackled with an exuberance that made Alexis wonder if the owner of the Ebbtide really was eighty years old as she'd been told.

"Well, I hope you'll forgive me for missing our scheduled appointment this afternoon, Miss Ferguson. I was looking forward to meeting you," Alexis answered.

"I can't apologize enough for what happened to you, but I can reschedule our appointment. I'm sure you'd like to relax after the ordeal you went through, so how about having lunch with me in the main dining room tomorrow? We can talk business at the same time." In a voice full of enthusiasm she continued, "Between now and then, I hope you'll feel free to enjoy all that the Ebbtide has to offer. We have a full selection of activities for our guests, you know."

"That sounds fine. I'll look forward to meeting you and talking about the Ebbtide's future. Will we be able to tour the hotel after lunch, Miss Ferguson?" She didn't want to sound too pushy, but she'd already lost a day's work.

"Certainly. I'll have it all arranged," the older woman agreed. "One more thing and then I'll let you go, as I'm sure you're exhausted. I have two other individuals who are interested in purchasing the hotel. We'll all meet for lunch together if it's all right with you." She chuckled aloud. "I had wanted to meet with each of you individually first, but unfortunately, our electrical problems prevented that."

"I certainly understand."

"Oh, one more thing I want to say to you, dear."

"Yes?" Alexis couldn't wait to meet this woman face-to-face. She sounded delightful.

"I intend to conduct the sale of my hotel in a forthright way. There will be no surprises."

"Thank you for telling me, Miss Ferguson. I'll look forward to tomorrow. Good-bye."

She hung up the telephone, wondering who the

other potential buyers could be. Oh, well, she told herself, why shouldn't there be others interested in the Ebbtide? It was a magnificent old structure.

Briefly, her thoughts returned to Harper Evans. He'd said he was here on business. She shook her head. Surely not. There wasn't one chance in a million that they'd both come to Galveston for the same thing.

Alexis set about making the room more homey, a trick she'd learned when traveling began to dominate her life. First she took out a silver-framed picture of her sister and herself standing on either side of a beautiful thoroughbred. It had been her sister's first win when she'd begun raising racehorses, and the picture didn't reveal who was proudest, Alexis or Abra. She rummaged around a little more in her suitcase and came up with a novel to read and her favorite slippers. After she had placed a call for fresh flowers, Alexis at last felt satisfied.

There was a light knock on her door, and she went to answer it.

"Ms. Cartwright?" the bellboy asked.

"Yes?"

"These are for you," the young man said, holding a vase of salmon-colored roses out to her. "I hope you don't mind ma'am," he continued, "but could you tell me if you're a Miss or a Mrs.?"

"You're efficient, but your question seems a little rude. Does the desk need to know this?" She was thinking how prompt the main desk had been in seeing that her flowers were delivered so quickly.

"He didn't say. He just said to come back and tell him."

30

"Who?" She looked at a card in the bellboy's hand and then glanced down the corridor as far as she could see. There was nothing there but two wide marble columns at the end of the hallway.

Confused, she shook her head. Then, out of the corner of her eye, she saw someone emerge from behind one of the columns. "He sent the flowers?" she asked, taking a step back.

"Wait, don't close the door." Harper Evans bellowed, bounding down the hallway until he was at her door. He slipped the bellboy some money and took the vase from his hand before dismissing the young man. "That's no way to treat a man whom you've injured."

He thrust the vase into her hands and smiled seductively as he leaned up against the doorway, narrowing the distance between the two of them. Once again, she could smell that same musky aftershave that seemed to be one of his trademarks. "I thought those were the flowers I'd ordered just a few moments ago." She smiled. "By the way, why is it important for you to know if I'm a Miss or a Mrs.? You've already asked me out to dinner, and I've accepted."

She caught him looking at her left hand before he answered her.

Harper rolled his twinkling eyes in mock disgust. "How can you even ask such a question? I've got to know what my chances are," he said in a playful-sounding voice. "I told you I'm in love, provided you can cook, of course. Have you forgotten already?"

"You're crazy. Do you know that? Absolutely insane."

"I wouldn't argue with a beautiful lady. Tell me, what color is your hair?"

She reached up and pulled out a curled strand, as if she were thinking about it, and then she let it go. He watched the way the curl clung and curved around her smoothly manicured finger and then fell back against her head in perfect order.

"Red, I guess. Reddish blond. I don't know," she answered honestly.

"Persimmon, tangerine, golden? I see all kinds of colors in it," he said softly as he stared down at her.

She felt a blush begin, and she was unable to stop its tedious climb along her neck and cheeks. "Thank you for the roses. They're lovely. I'm looking forward to seven o'clock." He was doing it all over again, wreaking havoc with her composure.

"That's what I've come to talk to you about," he began.

Disappointment struck her hard then, but she refused to admit it. "Oh, that's all right. If you have other plans . . . You didn't have to bring me roses."

"No, no, no. You're not getting rid of me that easily." He shook his head dramatically. "I thought we could meet for drinks at six and then have dinner. Hotel rooms bore me after a while. Don't they you?" He didn't wait for her to answer. "That gives you two hours to get ready." He started to walk away. "Same place. Don't be late. I hate it when women are late."

"You didn't even give me a chance to say yes or no," she called after him.

He nodded. "I know. I'm nobody's fool. Why don't you wear something peach, something to match those roses. I'd like that," he said over his shoulder.

32

The entire time she dressed, Alexis's thoughts kept returning to Harper Evans. He seemed bright, witty, and unpredictable. She couldn't deny that she felt a certain attraction to him, and yet she kept thinking about the possibility that they might be here for the same reason.

She began to daydream about what the evening might bring, totally aware of how good it felt to have someone as intriguing as Harper flattering her. She hadn't been near a man who was anything like him in a long time—perhaps too long—and a date for dinner sounded remarkably appealing.

Yet, as fun-loving as Harper Evans appeared on the surface, she suspected there was a very intense part of him somewhere hidden from view. A peculiar foreboding spread over her then, but she wasn't able to pinpoint the cause of her anxiety. She quickly thrust it from her mind, telling herself it was unimportant.

At five minutes before six, Alexis stepped out of her hotel room and locked the door behind her. She was wearing a pale blue silk sleeveless dress designed with faint tracings of color swirling along the fabric. The swirls were peach-toned, almost the color of the roses Harper Evans had given her. She'd chosen the dress as a concession to him while all the time aware of how well the pastel colors accented her smooth complexion and light blue eyes.

She wore perfectly round carnelian earrings trimmed in gold, and a matching wide bracelet of round stones. Since she'd broken her bottle of perfume earlier that day, she now wore none. Only the fading fragrance of her soap clung to her skin.

Unwilling to step into an elevator so soon after her experience, she strode down the stairs toward the main floor of the hotel and an evening with Harper Evans. As she walked, she looked the building over, making a mental note to write down the significant things she saw.

Alexis saw him watching her from the center of the lobby, and she sent him a tentative smile that grew in response to his own disarming one.

His greeting was a husky whisper. "Thank you for wearing those colors." He took her arm in his and walked with her across the lobby and into the bar.

She let him lead her away, once glancing up at him, wondering where his humor had gone. All the time she'd envisioned their greeting, she'd expected him to say something clever when he first saw her. But now she saw that there was a seriousness in his face she hadn't noticed before. The confidence with which he escorted her made her feel once again that there was far more to this man than what met the eye.

"Here we are," he said, pulling out a chair at a small corner table for her.

Over in one corner, there was a baby grand piano where a woman sat playing an old blues tune. Overhead fans stirred the air, and a cocktail waitress stood waiting to take their order. It was still early, so the bar was virtually empty.

Alexis wanted to take some time to study the details of the room, but she didn't want to appear distracted around Harper. She was interested in his somber attitude, a definite change from what she'd seen of the man earlier in the day.

"What would you like?" he asked, and patiently waited for her reply. Harper had watched Alexis come down the marble stairs of the old hotel, and she'd taken his breath away. With a blazing wreath of ginger-colored hair and an utterly confident manner, Alexis put most of the women he'd known to shame. Her totally self-assured manner made him think there was something special about her, and he vowed to get to know this woman very well.

"I'll take a glass of Chablis," she answered, looking around the room.

"Bring her a good Chablis, and I'll take Weller and branch water," he said, nodding to the waitress.

Harper produced a small, gift-wrapped box and handed it to Alexis. "What's this?" she asked.

"A little something I thought you might need after today," he replied, abruptly realizing he was thinking of how much he wanted to run his hands along the long, smooth lines of her throat.

Alexis looked at him again. "Seriously? I mean, you've already given me roses. That's more than enough. In fact, when room service sent up the flowers I'd ordered, I didn't know where to put them."

He let out a low, rumbling laugh of satisfaction and watched with amusement while she opened the package to find a bottle of perfume to replace the one she'd broken. It was Joy, her favorite fragrance, one that was expensive as well as difficult to find.

"Oh, Harper," she said, and impulsively reached over to squeeze his hand. When she touched him, she was struck by the obvious strength in his hand and let her own linger an instant too long.

"How on earth did you manage to get this so quickly?" she asked as she dabbed it behind her ears and on the pulse points of her wrists.

"I have my ways. Actually, I'd planned to exchange it for that secret weapon you attacked me with in the elevator today. I thought maybe before we started off sharing a drink and a meal you'd tell me precisely what it was you hit me with." An easy smile played at the corners of his mouth.

As the waitress brought their drinks, Alexis peered down toward the floor and then bent over. A puzzled expression covered Harper's face as she reached down and retrieved something.

Alexis tried to suppress a giggle. "My weapon." In her hand dangled a high-heeled shoe.

"You mean?" he asked self-consciously, reaching up to touch his head once again. His eyes widened, and an amused smile began to grow at the corner of his lips. "A lethal weapon! You had a lethal weapon and I could have been seriously wounded."

They burst into laughter, then he picked up his drink, and tapped his glass to hers in a toast. It was going to be a lovely evening, she decided as she looked across the table at Harper Evans. He had a marvelous sense of humor and seemed able to make her laugh at will. But even as he grinned at her from across the table, she couldn't miss the firm air of power and authority that he radiated. He'd make a formidable opponent; of that much she was certain.

Two drinks later they were still talking happily. It had been a long time since Alexis had been out with a man who seemed to take pleasure in her company the way Harper Evans did. He made her think she was not only an attractive woman but also entertaining and highly interesting as well. He didn't pry. He was a perfect gentleman, and when he took her hand in his as they walked into a small, intimate dining area behind the main dining room, she told herself she was glad to be with him. The madcap happenings of the afternoon had indeed led to something interesting.

"I thought we might enjoy this place for dinner. I'm sure there are many good restaurants in Galveston, but I'd like to find out how the food is here." Harper pushed her chair in for her.

"Wonderful. I'm glad you did," she answered with a brief smile. Alexis, too, was anxious to investigate the dining room—its atmosphere, service, and cuisine. She hadn't even realized there were two dining areas in the hotel.

"Then I thought we'd have coffee or an after-dinner drink out on the terrace later. We could even walk along the beach if you wanted to . . . as long as you part with your weapons before we go. I have no intention of walking anywhere with you if you're going to carry your shoes in your hand."

Alexis's eyes widened in mock surprise. "But without them I'd be defenseless," she taunted, caught up in the sheer pleasure of an evening out with such a man.

"Somehow I have trouble believing that. Anyway, my dear, it's the weapons or me. One time is more than enough." He looked down at his menu before adding, "In a lot of ways."

She watched the way his mouth turned down, effectively clouding the expression on his face. Now wasn't the time to ask him to explain himself.

"Let's order our food, and then I want you to tell me where you got that syrupy Southern accent. I think it's wonderful, but it's a little too heavy to be Texan."

Suddenly realizing she was ravenous, Alexis ordered a shrimp cocktail to be followed by prime rib with horseradish on the side. When he'd dismissed the waitress, Alexis answered, "My accent is easy enough to explain. My mother came from Georgia. If you think this is syrup, I'd like to hear you describe her speech."

"I thought you came from Texas," he quizzed her.

"I do, but my mother was born and raised in Georgia. She met my father at a horse show in Virginia and came back to Texas with him."

Harper raised one eyebrow. "After they were married, I assume."

"Of course."

"You know, my old grandmother would describe you as a real ritzy woman, and now I'm putting two and two together. You're not A. B. Cartwright's daughter, the man who dealt in silver and gold bullion, are you?" He eyed her speculatively.

"None other." She let her eyes trail up the lapels of his immaculately tailored, wheat-colored suit jacket, along the collar of his silk shirt, and then over the prominent lines of his strong face. Finally, she found herself looking into his dark brown eyes. "You recognized the name?"

"Shouldn't I?" His eyes held hers, blazing their way through her thoughts. "Now I know why they named you Alexis Bain Cartwright. ABC Investment Corporation." A huskiness lingered in his voice as he went on. "I've heard a lot of good things about your father. I've been in California for several years and haven't kept up with things back here, but I always heard he had a real head for business."

"Yes, I believe he did," she replied solemnly.

"Are you at all curious about me?" he asked after their main course had been served.

"Of course." Alexis wondered why he'd phrased his question that way.

"Good, that means you're interested," he said, sure of himself. "I'm from Frame Switch, Texas, and before you ask, I'll tell you where it is." Now he realized why she'd appeared so self-assured. As the daughter of one of the richest men in the world, she came by her aristocratic bearing naturally.

She started to laugh.

"You don't believe me, do you? Most people don't when I first tell them, but it's true. There is a town named Frame Switch. It has a Mexican restaurant, a one-room post office, and a gas station. I was born inside the gas station thirty-six years ago when my father was driving my mother to Austin to the hospital. Unfortunately, he had a flat tire, and that's how Frame Switch became my birthplace. I drove through there a year or so ago, but nobody remembered me."

She broke into laughter then. "Oh, that's wild. I love it."

The sound of her laughter filled him with pleasure. "Do you want to hear more?"

Looking down at her prime rib, Alexis nodded her

head, "Yes, but tell me one story at a time or I'll never finish my meal, and it looks awfully good."

"Okay, begin to eat," he said as he cut into his T-bone steak, his face glowing with satisfaction. Everything was going just as he'd imagined it would. Alexis Cartwright was as interesting as he'd thought she'd be, and the more relaxed she became, the more he liked her.

While she ate, Alexis took time to glance around the room. Walnut wainscoting ran up one half of the walls and was met by emerald green and gold wallpaper. Oriental rugs dotted the hardwood floors, and the room was cast in faint shadows by the play of teardrop lights from brass chandeliers. Muted strains of song could be heard from the other room.

"How is your prime rib? Is it good?" he asked her. She nodded. "And yours?"

"The meat's good, all right, but I'm sorry it's so noisy in here. The acoustics are terrible."

Alexis frowned. "I really hadn't noticed."

"I'm glad."

"You know, I've wanted to ask you this ever since we got out of that elevator this afternoon, Harper. How tall are you?" She sat back in her seat, admiring him. It was impossible not to.

His grin softened his features. He was accustomed to being asked about his height. "I'm six foot two."

"I thought you were even taller. I don't know why."

"I know. That's what everyone says. My mother always thought it was because of the way I walk. I guess I tend to walk a little straighter than most men. I worked several years lifting girders and concrete blocks, and my back always hurt, so I tried to walk straight. It helped me."

"You know, I'm not a short woman by any means, and you make me look tiny." The moment the words left her lips, she knew she shouldn't have said what she had.

He gave her a look that sent her pulse racing. Once again, some undefinable tension existed between them. Alexis had the same peculiar feeling as she had when he'd touched her earlier in the day. It caught her by surprise. Worst of all, she felt open and vulnerable to him.

"I'd love to see you in a pair of jeans. You'd look great, I bet." His eyes looked her up and down, his admiration unconcealed.

"Embarrassed by his compliment, she said, "You should meet my sister, Abra. She's two inches taller than I am, and she lives in jeans."

"We're making real progress, Alexis. So far you want me to meet your mother and your sister," he teased her, making her feel at ease again.

"Tell me more about yourself, Harper. You obviously haven't spent your life in Frame Switch."

"Let's see," he mused for a moment, taking his time. "I have a brother and two sisters and they're all older. I grew up on a farm outside Austin and went to college there. I worked my way through school in the construction business. Then, one day, I figured out that the men I worked for were buying buildings without putting much money down, and their monthly payments were paid by rent they received. I decided if they could do it I could, too, and so I saved my money and bought my first small building a couple of years after I finished college. That seemed so easy, I bought a few more, and so far so good," he finished modestly.

He didn't have to say any more about his business. She'd seen the way he dressed, looked at the Piaget watch on his suntanned wrist, and his handmade Italian shoes. He'd done very well for himself. She wanted to say something like, "Frame Switch must be proud of you," but she didn't. Somehow she knew he didn't like to draw attention to himself in that way.

And then it hit her—that same cloud of anxiety she'd felt earlier. Buying buildings, he'd said. Construction business? It was beginning to seem more and more as if they were both here for the same purpose. She hoped desperately that it wasn't true. She wanted more for the two of them.

"Would you like to take a walk along the beach?" His gaze locked with hers. "It's up to you."

She heard his words, but his look said so much more. If there was even a vague possibility that they both wanted to buy the Ebbtide, she knew she should say no and cut her losses here and now.

Taking a deep breath, banishing her doubts to some distant corner of her mind, she said, "Yes, I'd like that, Harper. I really would."

The night was still young, and the way he'd looked at her in that strangely intimate way earlier had made her pulse pound crazily. At the same time, it made her want to ride this out, to see what would happen. The feeling between them had been too strong, too intense to let it end until she was completely sure. She had always been a woman who took chances. There was no reason to stop now.

He stood and pulled her chair out. When she got up, he put his arm around her bare shoulders, his movements as natural as if the two of them had always been together. They both smiled.

Plunging into the warm night air outside the hotel felt good. Harper started to order drinks out on the terrace near the pool, but he suddenly changed his mind, convincing Alexis to take off her shoes and burrow her feet into the grainy sand for their promised walk.

The water shimmered with moonlight as they walked in comfortable silence. Each time a suspicious idea entered Alexis's thoughts, she coldly and effectively pushed it to the back of her mind. Harper couldn't possibly be a competitor. Fate wouldn't be that cruel.

A warm breeze whispered around them as Alexis said, "Earlier tonight you made a comment about once being enough for you. You said it in reference to my weapon, but I think you meant something else. You were referring to your wife, weren't you?"

"Ex," he said, nodding. "Now I know what you do for a living. You're a mind reader, a swami," he joked.

After a moment's pause, he continued. "Yeah, she and I got married when we finished college. It seemed to be the thing to do at the time. I started working hard. She started getting bored. We moved to California, and soon she was caught up in trying to be Mrs. Beverly Hills. When she stopped being faithful, I finally asked her to leave; there was nothing else to do."

They walked on. Alexis was aware of the profound silence. She was interested, immensely interested, in hearing what else he had to say.

"Anyway, when she left, she did it in style. She cleaned me out." He grimaced. "By the time she finished, my business and my bank account looked like Old Mother Hubbard's cupboard. She ended up with two of my finest vacation spots in California."

Alexis's head whirled at the implication of Harper's words. Vacation spots? Oh, no, it was impossible, surely!

He sighed softly. "But that was a long time ago."

She looked at him, trying to banish the possibility from her mind, but this time her thoughts stubbornly refused to leave. Everything Harper had said indicated that he was here to buy the Ebbtide.

He was waiting for her to say something, she could tell. After all, he'd just entrusted her with some very personal information about himself.

"Are you over it?" she asked.

"Yes, except, to tell you the truth, I still have a hard time trusting women."

All she could think about was one horrible possibility. He was her opponent! She was standing here, absorbed in intimate conversation, impatiently waiting for this man to stop their slow zigzag procession along the beach long enough to kiss her. And he was probably going to be her competitor by lunchtime tomorrow.

She took a deep breath. Why me? she longed to scream out. This can't be happening. Not now. Not

44

when I've found a man I want to spend some time with, get to know! Trust? If he only knew!

Suddenly, Alexis was acutely aware of his hand closed tightly around hers. There was something electric in his touch that surprised and confused her. She wanted to pull away from him, to sever all physical connection but couldn't bring herself to do it.

You're finding him much too attractive, she insisted to herself. This isn't going to get you anywhere, especially if he turns out to be tomorrow's opponent.

Her senses were on alert, and she was suddenly aware of everything about Harper Evans, everything she had seen. She knew she could close her eyes and trace from memory the almost forceful curve of his jaw, the beard line that was shaved to a smooth shadow, ending at the base of his cheek. Longing to touch his face, to explore with her hands, Alexis knew she would never be able to do so. The developing connection had to be broken.

The breeze once again whistled across the gulf, blowing a shock of Harper's dark brown hair across his forehead, giving him a boyish look that she found quite irresistible. But this was going to have to end, at least for the time being, until she found out whether he was here to buy the Ebbtide, too. If he was, she couldn't let him, no matter how much she liked him. The Ebbtide had to be hers.

"Why don't we head back?" she said softly, looking out at the calm gulf. "I'm afraid I'm going to have to ask you to excuse me. I'm really tired."

He squeezed her hand and turned with her, brushing his shoulder lightly against her arm as he did so.

"I'm the one who should be tired. After all, I was attacked today."

"You're lucky, actually. About a month ago I was planning to take self-defense lessons, but at the last minute something came up and I backed out." She shook her head poignantly. "Just think of the damage I might have done to you in that elevator."

In the cool night air, their laughter swelled out over the gulf. The moon had risen higher in the sky until it now smiled down upon them, and the sand felt soft beneath their feet.

"I'm still thinking about all the time we wasted in that elevator," he said solemnly.

"Forty-five minutes, at least," she replied.

"I'm not talking about that part of it." He slowed their pace down even more. "I'm talking about our being alone together."

She laughed, hoping he was kidding again, yet aware of the sensual pull that existed between them. She'd known it before, but never had it pulsed so fiercely inside her.

"The more I think about it, the better it sounds. I almost wish we were caught in the elevator again— now," he finished in a husky voice.

She tried to speed up their pace, but he held back. She kept looking straight ahead, trying to break the bond that she'd enthusiastically helped to create earlier.

"Well," he said softly.

"I don't know what you want me to say, Harper."

"Use your imagination," he whispered suggestively.

"You're making me blush again. That's not some-

46

thing I'm used to." She ought to tell him right now about her suspicions, but if she did, everything between them might be destroyed.

"That's good. It means you're thinking some of the same thoughts I am."

When he stopped and called her name, she shivered and, with a shy willingness that came as a surprise, closed her eyes, retreating from reality, back into the fantasy she'd been so comfortable with over the past few hours. His lips easily discovered hers, and suddenly she felt as if there were an invisible hand pressing hard against the small of her back, propelling her toward this desirable man. And all the time she knew she shouldn't.

Slowly Harper allowed himself to savor their kiss, telling himself that he would want to remember this moment for a very long time. Her mouth was softly pliant and sweet, and he moved his lips slowly and sensually against hers. The heat of her lips as he gently forced them apart struck a responsive chord in him, and his moist tongue entered her mouth to be received in ardent excitement.

He could smell the tantalizing fragrance of her perfume as the breeze blew it toward him from time to time. His hand inched up along her smooth, white throat, tracing the ridge of her neck until his fingers finally tangled in her blazing red curls. Ever so slowly, he ran his fingers through her hair over and over again.

Heat coursed through her veins as she responded to his touch, and she felt light and boneless, reacting to the intimacy of his fingers. Feverish, longing to be strong enough to resist her own urges, she reached up to bring her arms around his finely muscled back.

His lips played against her skin, nibbling at the outer shell of her ear and then moving in tantalizing slow motion to the tender flesh of her throat. Carefully, he memorized every spot his lips touched.

In spite of herself, Alexis found she was responding to his touch in a way that was totally new to her. She was willing to follow him anywhere, to do whatever he desired as long as he would continue to hold her and kiss her just as he was doing now.

Finally, his mouth moved away from her lips and she slowly opened her eyes. He kissed her cheekbones, her temples, and then her eyelids with a loving, muted caress of his lips, like a faint shadow falling across the evening sky.

Knowing that she must stop this until she found out if her suspicions were correct, Alexis pulled away, resisting the pressure of his hand against her back. There was no way she could mention the Ebbtide now. She'd let things go too far, and now she didn't know how she could get out of the mess she'd created with her own silence.

With a tantalizing slowness he brought his mouth back to hers, and she pulled back even though she ached to feel his moist tongue duel with her own. The chill of the night covered her, but she didn't notice. Alexis was only aware of what was happening inside her body and mind.

He looked at her, taking note of the way the moonlight shaded her heart-shaped face so that her round eyes seemed even more pronounced. His hard desire for her was tempered by his respect, and he assured himself that she was a very, very special woman. With a feathery touch he ran his fingers up and down the length of her arms.

His hands ran across her back and then returned to her side just below her breasts. He held her so distantly, so gently, that she felt a crazed surge of desire strike her, and she took a half-step forward, effectively connecting his hands to the warmth of her breasts. But despite the power of her desire, that peculiar sense of foreboding returned, weaving its way through her passion, and she pulled away.

But then he bent over her again, so close she could feel his silky breath against her face, and suddenly she was only aware of his lips against hers. He ran his tongue along the curved lines of her lip and then withdrew, bringing his teeth together to nibble tormentingly at her bottom lip.

Her senses reeled as this man brought new passions to life within her, passions she hadn't been aware existed. She clung to him desperately, feeling as if she could no longer even stand on her own.

Not wanting the night to end, but giving in to reason and the lateness of the hour, Harper gently pressed his forehead against hers. "Alexis Bain Cartwright, we must go in."

"I know," came her faint reply.

"Tomorrow night?" His head ached with the effort it took to pull away from her, but when he looked into her eyes, he knew he was doing the right thing. He wanted this to be more than a one-night liaison.

"We'll see," she answered, wishing the hours away, hoping against hope that when tomorrow dawned, she would discover that he was not here for the same purpose as she. Then they could resume what they'd begun.

He walked her to her room, and she vowed she wouldn't allow him to kiss her again. There had been too much between them already. He could arouse her desire far too easily.

"I'm warning you, Alexis. I'm a man who likes to court my women, to take things slow and easy."

She told herself not to answer, but she heard her voice saying softly, "And I'm a woman who enjoys being courted." Her throat ached with the urge to ask him what his business was here, to clear the air once and for all. But she'd already let far too much pass by.

"I've a feeling you're a woman who enjoys many things, Alexis, and being a man full of curiosity, I'd like to take the time to figure them out. How about swimming in the ocean at midnight? Do you like doing that?"

"I don't know. I've never done it before." She wished her heart weren't hammering so loudly.

He kissed her cheek, grazing her lips with his own full ones, and then stepped back, his fingers intertwined with hers. "Good. I like a woman who hasn't done everything. It leaves room for us to discover a few things together for the first time."

"You make it all sound extremely promising," she whispered faintly.

"Something tells me that it is. Let's both think about it until tomorrow night. Shall we?"

Alexis merely smiled and unlocked the door to her hotel room. She leaned against it when it was closed, listening to his muted footsteps as he walked away, praying with all her might that she was only a victim of her own rich imagination.

But an ominous feeling continued to haunt her. If he was here to buy the Ebbtide, the relationship that had begun so interestingly and developed so beautifully would be in jeopardy. All she could do now was wait and see who her companions would be for lunch tomorrow.

And if one of them turned out to be Harper, she didn't know what would happen. The Ebbtide was going to be hers, and nothing was going to interfere with her plans. She'd waited too long, worked too hard. It had to be hers!

Why, then, she asked herself, was she suddenly terrified of tomorrow?

CHAPTER THREE

Alexis kept drifting in and out of sleep, disturbed and troubled by her suspicions. She'd spent the first half of the evening thoroughly enjoying herself, steadfastly ignoring the vague uneasiness that kept overshadowing her. But finally, there were just too many indications that Harper was in the same business she was. She'd tried to control her responses but had only managed to get in deeper and deeper.

The next morning, as she sat drinking coffee ordered from room service and making extensive notes about the hotel, she realized she felt unusually nervous. If Harper should indeed turn out to be her primary adversary in buying the Ebbtide, Alexis knew he would be as strong an opponent as he had proven to be gentle and attentive the night before.

At eleven-thirty she dressed, choosing a white linen Bill Blass sheath dress that reminded her of a warm summer day. She began to dab on her perfume, and the scent of it evoked the memory of Harper's kiss all over again. She consoled herself with the reminder that the odds were overwhelmingly on her side. More than likely, Harper was here for a reason far different from the one she suspected, and after her meeting, she would be able to look forward to the night that was to come with him.

Picking up her briefcase, she carefully put her folder of notes, her architect's report, and all her other information inside before snapping it shut. Now was the time to concentrate on how she would obtain the glorious Ebbtide hotel. With loving hands she caressed the walnut railing on the wide staircase as she walked down the stairs, anxious to meet Sally Ferguson in person, ignoring the nagging doubt she felt about who her competition would be.

The dining room was crowded with noontime luncheon business. Alexis glanced around, hoping she'd recognize Miss Ferguson when she saw her. In one corner of the room was a raised platform with three steps leading up to it. On either side of the steps were two potted palms set in colorful, round, antique Chinese pots. The hotel manager she'd met the day before came up to her and reintroduced himself, asking her to follow him toward the carpeted landing.

Harper Evans sat next to the spry octogenarian he'd met a few brief moments before. He'd spent most of his morning looking at the building from the outside. His architect hadn't finished the preliminary report by the time he'd left Austin, so Harper had studied the foundation and roof lines on his own.

But during the night he'd had plenty of time to think about Alexis Cartwright. The woman was remarkably intelligent, with irresistible good looks. And she seemed to have the ability to draw him to her at will. There was something open about her, something that made him want to trust again. Con-

53

sidering what he'd been through, that idea alone was enough to make him ache to see her.

He heard his hostess ask if he'd care for a glass of wine or a drink, and then the old woman's voice faded away to be lost in the distant sounds of the room. Alexis stood in the doorway, a solitary figure that dominated his field of vision. Seeing her standing there in a white dress that clung so alluringly to her body, he forgot what he was doing and stood to walk over and greet her. Sally Ferguson would just have to wait.

"Mr. Evans?"

"Excuse me, won't you? I see someone I know," he said, stepping toward her even as she approached him.

He found himself smiling at her, not only with his face and eyes, but with his entire being, and it felt wonderful.

"Hello, Harper," she said in that soft voice that for him already held an unexplainable power.

"Miss Cartwright? Won't you join us?" Sally Ferguson stood next to her table with her hand outstretched in greeting, a pleasant smile lighting up her face.

A cursory glance told Alexis the woman acted and dressed the part of a person far younger than her eighty years. Her tailored suit was the color of winter grapes, and her white hair was cut in a short, becoming style. Alexis tried not to look at Harper as her gaze settled on the other man seated at the table. She could feel her body shaking with the realization that all her suspicions had been confirmed.

"Yes, well . . . I don't want to intrude," Alexis

54

replied sadly. The sharp disappointment flooding through her was made worse by the perplexed look on Harper's face.

Miss Ferguson smiled at each of them. "Miss Cartwright, please join us. I'd like you to meet Mr. Evans and Mr. Carson," she said, seeming not to notice the way Harper and Alexis stared at one another. "Let's discuss the future of the Ebbtide Hotel, my favorite place to be. Please." She made a gracious, sweeping movement with her arm and indicated where they were to sit.

"How do you do, Miss Cartwright." The man named Carson reached out and took her hand.

He was a well-dressed man, about fiftyish and balding. He shook her hand in a businesslike way before sitting back down next to Harper. Alexis allowed the hotel manager to seat her, barely noticing him when he walked away toward the kitchen.

Harper had been left speechless when he heard Sally Ferguson invite Alexis to join them. How in the hell had this happened? All of this was catching him by surprise, and he felt cheated, sure that Alexis had known somehow. She hadn't seemed surprised to see him at Sally Ferguson's table. Certainly she hadn't been caught off guard as he had been. He wondered if Miss Ferguson had told her about him or if she was merely a good enough detective to have added up the clues about his construction firm and his business interests.

"Miss Cartwright, Mr. Evans, here"—the old lady patted both their hands—"tells me he's been in the business of buying and selling buildings since he left college. Tell me about yourself."

Caught up in a whirlpool of churning emotions over this impossible situation, Alexis glanced at Harper. The black expression of animosity she saw on his face only increased her dismay. He was studying her intently, slowly running his finger along the edge of his wineglass.

Alexis winced. Harper was sizing her up, not as a woman this time, but as a competitor. He looked all business, cold and calculating, trying to figure out how formidable a rival she would make. She could see it in the depths of his dark brown eyes. She could also see a look of hurt and betrayal, or maybe it was just her own conscience.

"Now then, I'll begin at the beginning," Miss Ferguson proposed. "You, Miss Cartwright"—she nodded to Alexis—"and Mr. Evans and Mr. Carson have all contacted me about buying this hotel. As I told you yesterday on the telephone, I won't play games with any of you. I intend to keep everything on the up and up. I'll be as honest and forthright as I can be."

Alexis nodded her head mutely, trying to concentrate on what she was hearing. She wished there was some way she could still the tumultuous beating of her heart and stop the beads of perspiration that she felt forming along her hairline. She was afraid to pick up her water goblet for fear she might spill it.

Harper spoke up. "I'm very glad to hear that, Miss Ferguson. I'm afraid too many people among us have forgotten what the words *forthright* and *honest* mean. Dealing with you will be a welcome change."

He looked at Alexis, as if to drive home his message. Angered by his implications, she wanted to rail against the idea that two people who wanted the same thing had to be adversaries. She longed to find some way to deal with the situation, but it was already evident that that was impossible.

It was all Harper could do to keep himself from grabbing Alexis by the arm and forcing her outside to explain herself. I told her what I did for a living, he smoldered, but she never told me. If I hadn't pressed, she'd never have told me anything about herself. His cheeks blazed crimson. I told her about my life, and she just smiled that cagey female smile and suckered me in. Hell, she probably thought another day or two and I'd give her the damned hotel as a love gift!

Mr. Carson was saying, "The entire proposal sounds interesting." He looked at his two competitors. "A toast." He lifted his wineglass out in front of him. "May the best person win."

When they'd finished with the toast, in which Harper had reluctantly taken part, Sally Ferguson's voice crackled, "Now, let's have lunch and each of you tell me why you want to buy the Ebbtide." She let her eyes fall on each of them for a second. "I'm selling this hotel. It's too much for a person my age to take care of, and I've lived here too long to want to go through all the pains of having to fix it up. I've made up my mind. When I walk away from here, I don't care what you do with it. I'm finished with it, so don't think you have to sweet talk me about this old place. I'm ready to do business, and the highest offer is the one I'll take."

Harper was barely able to contain himself. He was enraged, recalling the conversation from the night before. She's one sharp lady, and I'll have to be careful.

He sipped his wine nonchalantly. The only good thing about what was happening, the only thing that made him smile, was the old lady's willingness to realize that the place wasn't worth saving. He'd never intended to lie to her about what would happen once he bought it.

"Where will you go?" Alexis responded to Miss Ferguson. She couldn't help but notice how quiet Mr. Carson was. He didn't involve himself in any of the conversation, and when she'd tried to engage him with her eyes, he quickly looked away.

"I have a house . . . a cottage, really, farther down the beach. I'll spend the rest of my life there doing all the things I've never had a chance to do since I took over this hotel. It will be a relief not to have to worry about anything more important than whether my tulips are growing well or not."

Alexis's insides felt like putty, but she held fast. At least, she reassured herself, she and Harper wanted the same thing. But she knew in her heart that she wanted it more. "I think this is one of the loveliest hotels around, certainly in this area. It must be restored." She couldn't bear to hear Miss Ferguson even raise the issue of destroying this priceless building. "What do you think, Harper?" she asked, trying to keep her thoughts on the business at hand.

His stare drilled into her. "I think that I've found myself in the most ironic of circumstances," he replied icily, "and the day is young."

"Mr. Carson, what do you think?" Alexis went on, ignoring Harper's jibe.

"I don't know, Miss Cartwright. We'll just have to see, won't we?" He didn't smile.

Two waiters delivered their luncheon plates filled with fresh, baked redfish and hush puppies. The men waited at the table for Miss Ferguson to dismiss them before they rushed away.

"The meal looks delicious, Miss Ferguson. I'm glad you chose to order for us." Harper smiled warmly at his hostess and was rewarded by a grin.

Everyone began to eat in silence, and after a few bites, Harper spoke again. "Just as I thought. It's delicious."

Mr. Carson nodded his agreement. Miss Ferguson motioned the waiters to refill the wine goblets.

Looking at Alexis, Harper couldn't stand the way she sat there, so self-contained and serene. "By the way, Miss Ferguson," he said pointedly. "I didn't tell you that Miss Cartwright and I met yesterday on the elevator, did I?"

Sally Ferguson shook her head, plainly absorbed in the attentions this handsome young man was giving her. "You don't mean you were on the same elevator when the power went out . . . ? How could you forget to tell me a story like that?" She looked as if she were having the time of her life.

"I guess it slipped my mind. I have a hard time remembering things sometimes, particularly depending on how important I think they are. Do you have that problem yourself?" He smiled.

"Indeed I do." She giggled and held up her glass of port. "A toast to the Ebbtide, your friendship, and all our futures. Now, you must call me Miss Sally. All my friends do."

Crossly, Alexis lifted her glass to theirs, unable to decipher all the emotions she was feeling. She'd had a shock, quite a shock, and Harper wasn't helping things at all with his sarcastic remarks. Feeling like a child who's just fallen off a merry-go-round, she wasn't certain whether she wanted to laugh or cry.

"Miss Ferguson, I mean, Miss Sally, have you had independent appraisals done of this property in the last six months?" Harper asked, alluding to the skyrocketing value of beachfront land for hotels. He'd spent a small fortune investigating the possibilities of beachfront properties along the Texas coast. This hotel was the only thing available, at any price, that suited his needs, and every grain of sand represented big profits.

Alexis looked at Harper's profile. He was talking animatedly, expertly manipulating the conversation, distinctly attempting to exclude her.

"Yes, I have, and all of you are welcome to look at them. I'll have them for you when we tour the hotel later. I hope you'll join me for dinner tomorrow night after you've had the opportunity to spend the day looking around and talking with your own appraisers. If you want to get into the spirit of the hotel, I'd suggest that you spend part of your time with our recreational director and his staff. Tomorrow they're planning a surfing contest, and it's always a big hit with our guests. We welcome everyone, young or old, experienced or novice. Our program's really quite exceptional," she said enthusiastically. "And then I plan to take you all out with me on my sailboat the next day."

Their conversation momentarily slowed while they ate. Alexis had lost her appetite, and the heavy port wine Miss Sally had ordered for them felt like a weighted piece of lead in the pit of her stomach. So far, the reality of what was happening was worse than her wildest expectations.

"Now, Mr. Carson, tell the others a little about yourself," Miss Sally insisted. "Let's get to know one another better." Before the man had a chance to answer, Miss Sally continued, "I plan to have fun with the three of you this week. This is an important occasion in an old woman's life."

Alexis smiled warmly at her, but as much as she admired Miss Sally's spunk, she just couldn't manage to revive her own. Why had she even bothered letting herself care about Harper's feelings? If he wanted to act like a Texas-size jackass, let him. She'd dealt with the toughest of men before and not been intimidated. The race was on.

"I own a real estate company here in Galveston, and I've had my eye on the Ebbtide for some time." Mr. Carson didn't change expressions but spoke in a flat monotone.

"And you, Mr. Evans, what about you?"

"I heard about the Ebbtide from a friend of a friend out in California, and since I was planning to move back to Texas, anyway, I thought I'd come to Galveston and take a look at the hotel. I've built several hotels in California, and I've had a great deal of fun with them." He gave Miss Sally a conspiratorial wink.

"Your turn, Miss Cartwright." The old woman beamed, still flush from Harper's attentions.

"Well, I'm from Houston, but I've been doing all my work in Oklahoma and Arkansas for the past few years, and I decided it was time to return to my home, too. I love this hotel. I love the name. I love the atmosphere. I intend to buy this little piece of history and restore it faithfully to its time."

"Oh, I knew this was going to be fun. I just knew it." Miss Sally then asked Mr. Carson a question before turning to Harper. "Mr. Evans, have you ever had the occasion to dine at the Four Seasons in New York City? They make a delicious white sauce there that I believe our chef prepares every bit as well. I'd like you to try it tomorrow night."

Alexis could tell that Miss Sally was quite taken with Harper's good looks and charming style. Being only too familiar with Harper's charm, she could certainly understand why Miss Sally kept directing her conversation his way.

"Miss Sally, I've eaten at the Four Seasons several times, but I'm sure their redfish couldn't be as delicious as this, and I look forward to sampling the Ebbtide's white sauce."

Like putty in his hand, Alexis thought, watching the way the Ebbtide's proprietor was responding to Harper. It didn't seem to bother Mr. Carson, she mused. He merely watched and listened, never changing his expression.

As they finished their meal, Alexis described how she would renovate the hotel. Miss Sally seemed quite interested in Alexis's proposals and seemed to get caught up in the younger woman's excitement. Harper elected to stay quiet while he fumed inside.

She was going to waste a fortune on this place if she got the chance to buy it. And then what would she have? An old building with new things piled on top of it to make it look good. The value of the property was in the land itself, but she didn't seem to know it. He wanted to throw his hands up in the air with disgust. She had to be a novice at this or much less intelligent than he had originally thought.

When they'd finished, Miss Sally escorted them all out of the dining room. "Let's start in the lobby, shall we? Or perhaps we should step outside and have a look at the place from the entrance." She grinned at them. "I'm trying to figure out how a realtor would start out this tour. There's a real knack to being able to show a place off to its best advantage, you know."

Alexis nodded agreeably, seeing Harper's brooding face out of the corner of her eye. It made her want to pinch herself, wake up from the bad dream she was living, and begin the day anew. But his attitude also served to steel her resolve to have the Ebbtide for her own.

Harper fought off the urge to tell Miss Sally that there wasn't much to show off, only a decaying old dream, and he respectfully kept quiet. It was all part of the negotiating, and he was accustomed to it.

"Follow me," he heard his hostess say to them, and he dutifully followed the two women and the quiet Mr. Carson out of the dining room, through antique doors, and caught a brief glimpse of himself in the beveled glass.

He looked like a fierce sea captain about to confront a tropical storm, and he tried to loosen up the scowl plastered across his face. Finding it impossible, he gave up. This was turning into one of the strangest days he'd ever spent. *I couldn't even dream this up!* he decided.

"Look, these doors alone are worth a fortune,"

Alexis said confidentially to Mr. Carson, who nodded indifferently. She'd made up her mind she'd act professionally despite the hard stares she kept getting from Harper. She wasn't going to let him interfere with her at all.

"Yes, but what would the termites do without them?" whispered Harper as he walked directly behind her. He knew those doors looked pretty, but they were too old and weatherbeaten to be effective. They'd bring a good price before the wrecking crew got to work.

"This place doesn't have termites," Alexis retorted, and turned around, glaring at him. She had a crazy desire to kick him in the shins. Her ire only increased when she noticed that Miss Sally and their adversary, Mr. Carson, seemed not to have heard Harper's quick little barb.

"What self-respecting termite would ignore a white elephant of a building like this one?" He gave her a curt grin and then turned back to look at the doors in question. "I bet they come from miles around, those termites. Probably invite their friends, too," he taunted airily. "Why don't we just lay it on the line and go up and ask our friendly hostess, who just happens to have a slight hearing loss."

Surprised, Alexis looked over at Miss Sally, catching for the first time the way the old woman kept her eyes on the face of the person she was talking to. It was true, and Harper had noticed it first. That made her even madder.

"I thought you were in construction," she charged when the others had gone out toward the grounds of the hotel. "I didn't know you were into exterminating and detective work."

He followed her down the outside steps. "If I'd been in the exterminating business I would have fumigated that elevator yesterday to get rid of the little rat that was locked in there with me. As for detective work," he said gruffly, "I'm no match for you in that department. You work and work to get your information, and all the time you say nothing about yourself. You just bat those little eyelashes around and zingo, you can find out anything you want to know."

"I did no such thing," she charged, aware of how they needed to catch up with the others, yet not caring. She wanted to reach out and strangle Harper Evans. "You're disgusting."

"Me?" He threw his head back and laughed. "What do you call a woman who'll use her feminine wiles on a man to get what she wants? Now, which one of us is disgusting, Miss Cartwright?" he taunted.

"Get away from me," she flared.

"Oh, I intend to, as soon as I get what I came for."

They caught up with the others and stood looking back at the front of the hotel. Harper eyed Alexis out of the corner of his eye for a long while, wanting to see what effect their argument had on her, but to his disappointment, she looked as calm and collected as ever. And the way her hair gleamed in the early-afternoon sun, a kaleidoscope of coppery colors, made him look away with a twinge of deep-felt disappointment.

"Miss Sally, have you ever had any deaths or calamities in this hotel? I'm curious," Harper asked in a low, husky voice, brushing a curl of brown hair away from his forehead.

"Umm, let me see." She stared skyward, her brow furrowed in deep meditation. "Yes, I believe we did have one . . . no, two calamities. Once in the 1920s a man died in his bed with a heart attack and then in 1943, I believe it was, a woman shot her husband up on the eighth floor. He was with someone else, you see."

"So there is a touch of scandal locked away in the walls of the Ebbtide? I already knew there was intrigue." He shot Alexis a cutting grin.

Miss Sally gave him a vague look, not understanding what he was referring to, but when he smiled at her, Alexis saw the warm response in the woman's eyes. Alexis had caught the intent of his words, and she looked forward to the moment when she could throw him out of the hotel, her hotel. She took her sunglasses from her purse and put them on. She didn't want even to look at Harper any more today.

Taking charge, Harper started back toward the hotel. The others followed him until they came to a fountain that was set out about four feet in front of the entryway.

"What a marvelous fountain," Alexis exclaimed. "I noticed it when I came in and stopped to admire it then. It's wonderful; you don't find craftsmanship like this anymore."

"Yes," Miss Sally nodded, leading them to the front doors again.

"Thank God for that," Harper added smoothly in passing as he looked at the six carved cupids spitting water.

Busy with the appraisal sheets she had in her hand, Miss Sally hadn't heard him, but Alexis had.

"Now, the Ebbtide was built in 1890 and opened in the spring of 1891. The foundation is made of thick cypress logs, completely termite-proof and as strong as the day it was built."

"Oh," Alexis said admiringly before glancing at Harper, her eyebrows raised as if to say, "I told you so."

Harper looked out at the distant skyline in disgust. Cypress-tree stumps? A foundation that was older than Methuselah and here she was oohing and ahhing about it like it wouldn't cost a fortune to replace. I'll bet there isn't a level room in the building, he told himself.

"When was the last time you had the foundation inspected?" Harper asked, growing increasingly irritated with Alexis's uncritical approach to the hotel.

"I'm really not sure. Let's look on the appraisal in a moment and see if there's any reference to inspections and dates."

"Actually, Miss Sally's probably correct about the cypress-tree stumps. They have a natural resistance to termites," Alexis offered, rubbing salt in the wound. And when she began citing facts and figures to substantiate her own judgments, Harper had to admit that he admired the depth of thinking, if not her thoughts.

"This wooden porch was made to encircle three sides of the hotel," Miss Sally went on when Alexis was finished. "Many of our visitors love to sit here all day long. We keep game tables, a portable bar, and a television discreetly hidden away to be taken out only for important happenings like football games and things."

"I'd like to spend some time like that," Harper spoke up, eyeing the rotting spindles on the railing. "I spend all my time working, so I don't have much chance." His irritation was building to a hard boil of frustration. Couldn't Alexis see how foolish she was being about the place?

"You have the whole week now, so take advantage of it," Miss Sally replied.

"You're right," he confirmed, unable to stop himself from wondering just how much money was spent to maintain this fine old porch. As inconspicuously as possible, he walked over to the rotting section of railing and idly fingered it, hoping Alexis would see what he was doing and take notice of why, but she was following right behind Miss Sally.

"Next we'll go to the main desk."

Alexis, Harper, and Mr. Carson followed the spry woman through the lobby, each absorbed in their own separate thoughts. Alexis wondered why Harper was so quick to find fault with the hotel. Was it because he wanted to drive the asking price down, or was it because he saw how much she loved it already?

Harper grimaced. He could easily see that she was thoroughly taken with the place, and the very idea of it twisted his frustration into mounting anger, making him shamelessly consider trying to keep it from her. He had to admit to the fact that he'd been crushed when he'd discovered her deception of the previous night. Alexis had seemed interested in him but obviously had wanted only to discover his plans for the hotel. He'd wanted so damned desperately to trust this woman, and she'd turned out to be completely untrustworthy.

"Many of our operations are still done in an Old World manner," Miss Sally was saying. "We favor the European style of hotel management. Our costs are a little greater because of the number of additional personnel we employ, but we feel it's well worth it. We have created a certain ambiance that brings our guests back year after year."

Alexis nodded. "That's one of the things I've often heard about your hotel, Miss Sally. If I buy the Ebbtide, that's the tradition I'll maintain. Frankly, I believe it's one of your strongest selling points."

"Thank you, dear."

"That's a pretty costly consideration, if you're really interested in making money at this," Harper interjected.

"Of course I'm interested in making money in this venture."

"Oh, really. That's interesting to know," he replied dryly.

He wasn't the same man she'd been with the night before. Not at all. He wasn't even the same man she'd had lunch with. It was as if with each step of their tour he was becoming increasingly tense and distant. Alexis didn't understand anything about him right now. All she could ascertain from her quick glance was a cold, set look on his face. He kept his eyes fixed at a point beyond her.

"The manager has a comfortable office directly behind the main counter, which, incidentally, is made of hand-carved rosewood, as are the cubbyholes back there that hold the keys and messages for our guests." Miss Sally escorted them both around the counter and into the manager's office. "We have a staff lounge in the back where the bellboys and other downstairs staff take their breaks, get their messages, and so forth."

Harper paid little attention to what she was saying. He was already thinking ahead.

Alexis rubbed the counter with her hands, feeling the warm, smooth surface of the wood. She could hardly pay attention to Miss Sally's words; she was too busy trying to figure out how she could have this hotel for herself. She could imagine what the Ebbtide could be made to look like with the proper remodeling. Now more than ever she knew she had to have it.

"How many employees do you have, Miss Sally?" Harper's deep voice cut into her thoughts.

"We employ split shifts of fifty each. Two groups, so that makes about a hundred people all together. Sometimes we hire more for busy holidays and all."

"Have you told your employees that you're selling the hotel?" He stood in the doorway of the manager's office, effectively filling the space.

"Yes, Mr. Evans. I met with them yesterday. That's why I had asked each of you to keep everything hush-hush before now. I wasn't quite ready yet to announce it." She lifted her head up and sniffed. "Now I am, and so they know."

"Good," he acknowledged, and walked on ahead of them, catching sight of the damaged wainscoting in the hallway and the dim lighting. He gave the ceiling a quick, critical study and looked back over his shoulder at Mr. Carson to see if he'd noticed the flaws also, but he gave no indication he had.

70

Miss Sally took them to room 211, citing it as a typical example of what the rooms of the Ebbtide looked like. Harper told himself if he heard Alexis rave about the charming atmosphere one more time he'd burst. It was getting to be too much for him, this infatuation of hers. He looked at the old hotel and saw red ink on an accountant's ledger. It seemed that she looked at it and saw something out of a fairy tale. In his estimation, that was absolutely ridiculous.

"One half of our rooms have two double beds, one fourth have kingsize, and one fourth have twins."

And I'll bet every last one of the mattresses is as lumpy as hell, Harper wanted to add.

"When did you last replace the mattresses?" Alexis asked, pulling a note pad and pen from her purse. Too many things needed to be remembered now if she wanted her bid to be well estimated. She wondered how Harper and Mr. Carson managed to remember everything, especially when both men seemed so far removed from what they were doing.

The mattresses were replaced right after the First World War, Harper chuckled to himself, as Miss Sally answered Alexis. He walked to the window and looked out so that they couldn't see his face. When they left the room and headed toward the elevators, Harper trailed behind them, wondering how long this could go on.

Listening to Miss Sally's discussion of the hotel's maintenance program, Harper bit his tongue to keep quiet. The way Alexis was going on about it was too much. She acted as though a hundred and fifty thousand dollars for a completely new elevator system was nothing.

"You know it would cost a great deal of money to do all the things that so obviously need to be done around here," he said, determined to make his point. Damn it, what was this obsession Alexis had about restoring this hotel?

"I do realize that," Miss Sally agreed as she stepped out of the elevator and led them down the galley into the kitchen. She took Mr. Carson over to speak to the headwaiter. They obviously knew one another.

"I don't think the renovation costs would be excessive. Not when you compare them to new construction costs." Alexis stood outside the kitchen, her face shaded by the dim hallway light.

"Obviously, we don't see eye to eye," Harper said in open challenge. "Our values are very different."

"Okay, Harper, let's get all of this out into the open." She flushed angrily.

"You couldn't be open if your life depended on it. I ought to know. I found out firsthand."

"Look"—she waved her hand dismissively—"I've just about had it with you and your rude remarks. I think we should discuss the problem between us—and soon. I'm sure Mr. Carson and our hostess are not interested in our differences, but I can't put up with this much longer."

He drew himself up to his full height, straightening his shoulders before breathing a deep sigh as he towered over her intimidatingly. "I don't care what Mr. Carson is interested in," he hissed. "And Miss Sally hasn't even heard or noticed, so I'm not feeling any concern about either one of them."

He put his arm up against the narrow hallway

wall, effectively walling her off from the entrance to the kitchen. "We have no need for any further discussion. You've had your shot at me, and once is enough!"

"All right then, I suggest you at least try to behave in a more businesslike manner," Alexis challenged.

"Me?" he croaked. "You're running around here acting like Cinderella at the prince's palace, the picture of innocence. But you and I both know what a little schemer you are. A schemer as well as a seducer."

"Get out of my way," she retorted in a choked voice. Her eyes blazed and she hurried ahead, fighting the hostility that seized her.

"Here we are," Miss Sally said when they'd caught up with her. She then introduced everyone to the chef, who had to wipe flour from his hands before he could greet them properly.

The kitchen was well stocked with copper pans hanging overhead and a long, narrow work area in the center of the room. Tantalizing odors rose from the stove, on which pots were boiling with food.

Compared with all else he had seen, the kitchen was the only area that Harper couldn't find lacking. The kitchen in the last hotel he'd built had a better design but he couldn't really fault this one. He made a mental note to see if the chef was interested in a new job. He looked efficient.

"You know, I really think this kitchen is exceptional," Alexis told them all, regaining her composure, despite Harper's outburst. Oh, sweet revenge, come to me, she thought.

Miss Sally walked on toward the back. "I'll let you look around here for a few minutes."

"This is the best spot to leave prospective clients. She's handling all of this exactly like a good realtor would," Harper muttered. "This is by far the best place on this haunted-house tour." Harper noticed Mr. Carson's attempt at a feeble smile and watched as the man strolled off toward the outer door.

That was the last straw. Drawing her hands to her hips, Alexis was ready to do battle. "Haunted house?" she snapped. "This is one of the loveliest hotels in all of Texas, and you call it a haunted house?"

"That's putting it politely." Might as well get it all out in the open he decided, before he choked on it.

"You're unbelievable!" She said the word as if it were a terrible insult.

"I prefer unbelievable to ridiculous!"

"Just tell me why you're here if you think this hotel is so bad," she insisted, never taking her hands away from her hips.

"Listen, you two." Miss Sally came up behind her. "I hate to do this to you, but I have a problem that needs my attention right now, a little plumbing problem. I had planned to give you a tour of the basement and show you my books, but I'm afraid it will have to wait. Mr. Carson has to leave. Please excuse me, won't you? We'll meet again tomorrow night. Meanwhile, keep looking around, and feel free to take part in the hotel activities." She smiled and reached out to shake Alexis's hand.

When she gripped Harper's, she stopped and looked directly at him. "Mr. Evans, please don't think you have to humor an old woman. If you intend to tear down this hotel, feel free to discuss it. As I told you before, once it's sold, I'm through." She contemplated him with wise eyes. "All through."

"Thank you. I'll remember that," he answered with satisfaction.

Watching the old woman walk away, Alexis could feel anger welling up inside her. She was so furious, she thought she might cry. She swung back around to face him. "Tear down this hotel? Did she say tear down this hotel?"

The look in Harper's eyes was answer enough.

"You don't honestly mean you intend to tear down this beautiful place? This is history. Can't you see that? Doesn't that mean anything at all to you?"

"I came to buy this hotel. I don't think I have to explain anything or justify myself as long as I'm the highest bidder." His implication hovered in the air between them.

"Oh, I see. You merely want the property. Is that it?" She stepped toward him until they stood in the center of the cooking area.

"Yes, that's it," he shouted back, moving to meet her. "And while we're on the subject, Miss Alexis Bain Cartwright, you're acting like I'm doing something wrong. Well, I know I'm not the fool in this deal."

The cooks, dishwashers, and waiters who happened to be in the kitchen when their voices began to rise stood watching them, but Alexis was too distraught to let it disturb her. She only felt the clamoring of her own fierce rage.

"Fool? You think I'm the fool for wanting to renovate this hotel? Oh, come now. A fool is someone who doesn't know what he's doing . . . or what he's destroying." Her blue eyes widened in accusation. "I think that takes me out of the running." Her breath came hard and fast now, and she could feel her heart beating wildly.

"Ha, just because I don't want to throw away good money trying to save this old relic, you think that's wrong?" He clenched his strong hands into fists as the two of them stood eyeing one another warily. Alexis had to strain to look up at him, he was standing so near.

"You don't understand or appreciate anything about history or preservation of heritage, do you?" she sputtered.

"Oh, now, it's old flag day. Am I being unpatriotic just because I want to build a hotel that will make money? Free enterprise—that's the name of the game. Remember?"

"There's a way to make money and preserve a little part of history, Mr. Evans. It seems that many people have forgotten that, but it's true. This is not the place for chrome and glass. Not here."

"Have you ever done a cost-effectiveness study on remodeling an old, dilapidated structure like this one?" he asked insolently.

"I have several hotels just like this one."

"Then you have my sympathy." He glowered. "You ought to know that you can't make money patching up stuff. It simply will not pay off. Repairs and maintenance alone will eat you alive."

"All I know," she persisted, "is that in the past it has paid off for me."

"Maybe as a tax write-off, for all the millions you've inherited." He let a knowing grin play along the corners of his mouth.

Furious now, she was willing to do almost anything to wipe that grin off his face. "No, I mean in the black, a profit, Harper. P-R-O-F-I-T!" she almost screamed.

"I know how to spell, thank you."

Sharply, she looked at him, full of anger and skepticism, unable to stop the flow of her own words. "And another thing, I've never used family money for my hotels."

"Oh, come on, Alexis. Do you expect me to believe that line?" he jeered. "That silver spoon you've got hanging out of your mouth looks a little crooked, Miss A. B. Cartwright. Don't ask me to believe that hogwash." His old Texas drawl returned as he raised his voice.

"Frankly, I don't care what you believe. I know the facts," she replied, quite affronted.

"Look, lady, it's as simple as this. I'm talking business—practical, realistic, profit-and-loss business. You're talking entertainment. You probably see yourself as Scarlett O'Hara coming down those steps."

"You have a real mean streak in you, don't you?"

"I'd say we're evenly matched," he announced blandly. "You didn't even bother pretending to look surprised this morning," he challenged, his voice slowing as he changed the subject. "When we were out there on the beach last night—you knew it, didn't you?"

"No," she answered without elaborating.

"Liar."

"Name-calling doesn't become you," she replied crisply.

He stared deeply into her eyes, and she could feel the tension between them so intensely that she felt herself consumed by it. But there was no time for reflection now. She was operating on pure instinct.

Ignoring her gibe, he continued to taunt her. "This is one time Daddy's money isn't going to buy you what you want, lady!" he snapped excitedly, his face reddening with anger. "I'll have this place. You'll lose."

"Oh, that's very doubtful. Don't underestimate the competition."

"I thrive on competition. Real competition, that is. Too bad I don't have any. Mr. Carson looks easy, and you . . . you're no serious threat."

"We'll see about that. I doubt you'll be acting quite so arrogantly when we're all through here."

"We are through here. You might as well throw in the towel, Miss Cartwright, because you're just wasting your time."

"You're wrong, Harper. I'm the one who's going to own the Ebbtide."

"Over my dead body!"

"What kind of flowers shall I send?"

"Don't bother. There's nothing I want from you." He studied her for a second longer. "If you think for one minute," he said in a slow, hard voice, "that I'm going to roll over and play dead simply because a woman I'm attracted to wants the same thing I do, you're very naive. I didn't get where I am playing kids' games."

Her eyes smoldered as she stepped closer to him.

"Neither did I, but don't worry about it. The attraction was entirely imaginary. In fact, I think it's safe to say that we have absolutely nothing in common."

"That's the first right thing you've said all day long, Alexis. I don't know what I saw in you yesterday. I guess it was the blow on the head."

"Oh, I doubt it. It would have taken someone a lot stronger than I am to put a dent in your hard head!"

"I'll give you fair warning. I'm going to buy this hotel." He took deep, quivering breaths, knowing he was losing control but unable to stop himself.

"You're wrong," she said simply as she turned and stalked away, aware only of a crushing feeling of despair within her.

She didn't even bother to look back when she heard the sound of clapping hands from behind her. The kitchen staff had enjoyed the show, and she didn't give a damn. Her whole being, body and soul, was filled with her own sense of self-preservation. But why does it hurt so much? she asked herself. Why?

CHAPTER FOUR

It took Alexis the entire night and most of the next morning to still her rage. She had given herself over to it completely. It had been a long time since she'd allowed herself to become quite this angry, but this time she just couldn't help it.

Intent upon having a personal inspection of her own, Alexis spent the late morning poking around the Ebbtide, looking at everything from the electrical wiring to the antique furniture in the lobby. Occupying herself with an intense study of the hotel was a dusty and time-consuming job, but it didn't stop her thoughts from returning to Harper Evans and the events of the past two days.

When she saw him talking to a woman outside the hotel near the kitchen delivery entrance, she turned and started back toward the front of the building. Seeing him only reminded her of her own foolishness in allowing herself to become involved in such a bizarre situation. She hurriedly started to rush away, hoping he hadn't spotted her.

"Alexis," Harper called.

She hadn't gone far enough away to pretend she hadn't heard him. Warily, she turned around. "Yes?" After their battle in the kitchen the day before, she'd imagined they might not even bother speaking to one another, but that would be a childish act.

"I'm curious." Harper walked toward her, leaving his companion behind holding what looked like blueprints.

Alexis looked longingly at the front of the hotel and then at him. There was no escaping their meeting, and so she stood watching the way the breeze from the gulf played with his hair, swirling it to and fro. His navy blazer flared out from his sides as he approached her, and his face held a grim expression that warned her he would have nothing good to say. She slowly began to tap her foot in a not-so-subtle show of impatience.

"You say you're curious, Mr. Evans. Am I supposed to ask why?"

He continued toward her, looking as if he might not stop when he got there, but she stood her ground. The glare of the sun made her frown.

"Not necessarily. I intended to tell you, anyway." He stood so close, his body shielded her from the bright sunlight, and he watched as her frown faded away. He cleared his throat. "I'm curious. I mean, I really am curious to know something."

"I understand," she said mockingly. "You're curious."

Ignoring her remark, he went on, "Have you even bothered checking out the integrity of the structure? I mean, do you use any resources to make your judgments about these old buildings or do you merely shut your eyes and picture what millions of dollars can do for the old place?" His gaze moved up until he was staring at a loose rain gutter dangling from the roof of the hotel.

"Well, now you have me curious, Mr. Evans. Is this the kind of thing you think about in the middle of the night—whether I bother checking out building structure—or do you spend most of your time thinking up rude remarks?" Her voice was cold and flat.

"It would probably surprise you if I were to tell you." He stared at her.

"In that case, don't bother yourself about it. The question can wait." Irritated with him, she went on. "Since it disturbs you so, Mr. Evans, I'll tell you how I operate. I wait until after midnight, then I take my crystal ball and my witch's powder and go out on the beach where I chant up at the moon, and poof, before you know it, all my questions are answered." She smiled haughtily at him, and her tone became serious. "Of course I study the structure, along with everything else about a building. Probably just as much as you do."

"Meet my architect, Harriet Winslow," he said to her as the woman he'd been with approached them. "Harriet, this is the woman I was telling you about, Miss Alexis Cartwright."

"How do you do," the architect said softly, shaking Alexis's hand.

"It's a pleasure to meet you." Alexis wondered exactly what Harper had told Harriet Winslow about her but then decided she really didn't want to know. It would probably make her angry all over again.

"I was about to—" Harper began.

"Excuse me," Alexis interrupted. "I know it's very

rude of me, but I am on a very tight schedule." She started backing away. "I hope you'll excuse me."

"Certainly." The woman smiled cordially.

"I know how you could save yourself some time," Harper said, taking a step toward her. "Don't waste it bidding on this old hotel."

Meeting his challenge, Alexis stared straight into his eyes. "You must be joking." Then, not waiting for an answer, she nodded to his companion and turned to leave.

"No, not at all," he replied, walking along with her. The architect had gone back to studying her blueprints.

"I've made up my mind. You know that." She picked up her speed. "We don't have anything more to talk about."

"You ought to let my architect talk to you," he persisted, keeping up with her. Seeing Alexis had made him forget his private vow. He'd decided to have nothing to do with her again, not after she'd toyed with him the way she had. Too late, he'd allowed his anger and frustration to override his good sense.

She didn't bother trying to conceal the indignation in her voice. "Now why on earth would I want to do that?"

"Because she happens to know a great deal about hotels. That's why."

Finally, Alexis turned toward the front porch of the hotel, out of earshot of the architect. "I am not interested in hearing any opinions from your architect, and it has nothing to do with her or her qualifications. I'm sure she wouldn't be interested in the kind of hotel I'm going to have here."

"How do you know that?"

Alexis stopped where she was, put her hands on her hips, and looked directly into Harper's eyes. "Because she works for you. That's why."

"You sure ought to listen to somebody."

Her voice began to rise more with each word she spoke. "If I want any help from you I'll ask for it. If I want to hear your opinions I'll ask for them, and if I want any advice I know where to get it!" She started to leave.

"Okay, but don't ever say I didn't try to help you. Some people just have more money than brains."

"You're the most opinionated, pigheaded man I've ever met," she said, her voice quivering with suppressed fury. "Why on earth can't you leave me alone?"

Suddenly, she was literally shaking with anger. Why, she asked herself, was it so disturbing to her that this man's values were so diametrically opposed to her own, and why was it so important to her that she let him know she was a success without her family's money?

"When you thought I might help you, you didn't seem to want me to leave you alone."

"Do you really want to discuss this?"

"No." He sneered. He didn't want to discuss anything at all with her, so why had he practically chased her down, trying to get his point across? Harper turned and stormed back to his architect, and as he went, his anger turned inward. He'd made a damned fool of himself. Again.

Alexis called room service for lunch, insisting to herself that she was eating in her room simply because it was the most expedient thing to do. Finally, though, she had to admit that the real reason was that she was unwilling to risk the possibility of seeing Harper again. The morning episode had rekindled all her feelings of confusion and anger.

Angry at herself for letting down her personal barriers so easily with a stranger, Alexis wondered how she could have involved herself so quickly and easily with a man like Harper Evans. She hadn't trusted him even before she'd been able to see him in the elevator, and she'd been right.

She ate her club sandwich while trying to study a preliminary report her own architect had sent with her. She made a few notes and, after checking the time, put her papers back into her attaché case. Miss Sally had mentioned the surfing contest that was planned for the afternoon, and Alexis decided to join in the activities.

When she had put on her black, two-piece bathing suit and thrown on a black terry-cloth crop top to cover it, she went downstairs, so intent upon her plans that she forgot her misgivings and took the elevator for the first time since the accident.

The moment the doors closed, she froze, recalling her resolution to avoid this mechanical horror until she could buy the hotel and have it fixed. As she began the slow descent to the lobby, she listened attentively to the familiar creaking and groaning of the equipment. There was something about the elevator that made her feel as though Harper Evans were still with her. The scent of him was there, that rich, musky essence that she remembered from the time they'd been trapped together.

One thought led to another, and suddenly Alexis found herself remembering his warm kiss and the tender way he'd let his lips touch her own. Then she recalled her own almost violent urge to make love to him that night out on the beach. By the time the elevator stopped on the first floor, she felt a new wave of confusion sweep through her. Those memories weren't bad, she realized with a jolt. They were beautiful.

"Miss Cartwright, will you be joining our surfing competition?" The hotel manager stood at the front door, helping the guests, answering questions and showing them the designated spot on the beach where the surfboards had been arranged and hotel employees waited to organize the games.

"I think I will," she answered with a smile.

"That's good. Miss Sally will be so pleased. These activities were all her idea, you know. In fact, she led the very first one, years ago." He glanced thoughtfully out the door at the growing crowd. "I think I'll call her and tell her to watch for you."

"That's very thoughtful of you." Alexis was pleased to see the way the manager handled himself with the guests, and she made a mental note to find out a little more about him. He might be the key to the transition of the hotel.

"Why don't you go to instructor number two. He's a fine teacher and a very helpful young man. You'll see the number painted on a board right out there where the group is standing. Good luck."

"Thanks."

Alexis hurried out the door and down the steps, feeling the breeze pick up as she went. Once she stepped onto the sandy beach, her pace slowed, and she watched until she saw a small board painted with a bright blue number one. She passed it and walked toward the next one, accidently dropping her sunglasses as she approached her assigned spot.

"Hey, I think you dropped something." A young man wearing a red cap with a picture of the Ebbtide on it reached down and scooped up her glasses.

"Thank you," she said.

"Are you participating in the competition? We're going to get started in just a few minutes, and we welcome all the entrants we can find." He smiled down at her.

"Good. I'm anxious to see how this contest works."

Out of the corner of her eye, Alexis caught a glimpse of a man running his hand along the lower surface of a surfboard. The man had his back turned to her and wore a rust-colored bathing suit and a matching cotton T-shirt. She couldn't see his face, but from the cut of his hair and the way his body filled the suit, she knew without a doubt it was Harper. Her head began to pound. She'd never dreamed he'd be here.

Harper heard that soft Southern voice and knew immediately who it was. Slowly he turned around. "Oh, no," he murmured to himself.

Alexis shot him an angry look and then asked the

instructor, "Is there another group I might join? I think you have your hands full."

"Oh, no. I'm happy to have you with us. We need a few more, in fact. I'll be right back." The instructor ran toward another young man wearing a red cap.

"Well, I'm leaving," Alexis said.

"That figures."

She watched as Harper moved closer to her, a surfboard tucked under one arm. Trying to decide what she should do, Alexis attempted to ignore the way his muscles stood out as he carried the surfboard, making it seem as light as a stick. His T-shirt covered his chest, but a shadow of coarse hair curled at the neckline of the fabric. She forced herself to look away.

"I said, that figures." He stood next to her now, facing her.

"I heard what you said." She spun away, making up her mind. She was definitely leaving.

"You're the kind of woman who'll be mad when I win, even though you won't compete," he called out, a little too loudly.

Alexis stopped where she was, feeling the way the sand covered her toes. "I beg your pardon?"

"I was right yesterday," he baited her. "You're not going to be much competition."

Her eyes glinted angrily as her thoughts returned to the times she'd surfed when she was a young girl. It should be just like riding a bicycle, she thought. Just get back out there and it will all come back to you in a rush. It had been a long time, but so what?

"We'll see who's not going to be much competition," she retorted, retracing her steps. "Just you watch."

He caught the change in her expression. Harper knew he should try to stay away from her, let her go, but he wanted to prove something to her. He couldn't be quiet. Suddenly, she was grinning at the idea of the challenge, and it excited him.

"Oh, I intend to watch, all right," he said, returning her smile. "I can hardly wait."

"You know, I'm beginning to believe there's only one way to shut you up, Mr. Evans."

"Oh? And you have the answer?"

"Yes, to show you once and for all that I'm out of your league, whether it comes to surfing or buying old hotels."

The instructor walked back to where they stood, talking as he walked. "Okay, folks. We're all ready to begin. Here's how we do it. The object is to watch for a good wave and go for it. We've got spotters out on rafts, and they'll be the judges." He motioned them to follow him toward the shoreline. "The object is to get a good wave and ride it all the way in. The winner will be selected by how far and how long they ride. If you haven't done it before, I'm going to be helping you. Don't hurry. We've got all afternoon."

"You need a surfboard," Harper snapped at Alexis. "You can't do this without one."

"That's right. Pick out the one you like." The instructor nodded politely. "We'll wait for you."

Fuming, Alexis walked back to where the surfboards were stored, vaguely aware of the noise of laughter and conversation coming from the groups scattered around them. That's why she'd come out here, to have fun. One part of her wished she could just keep walking—all the way to the hotel—while another wanted to pick up the surfboard and swing it across Harper's backside.

Giving the boards only a cursory inspection before selecting one, Alexis adjusted her sunglasses and hurried back to where the other competitors stood. Two more people had joined their group, introducing themselves to her as they went for their surfboards.

"No, I've never done this before," she heard Harper telling the instructor.

Harper had his surfboard standing upright next to him as if he were planning to use it at any moment. Immediately, Alexis was on edge. It wouldn't do to have him beat her out. This was her chance to show him a thing or two.

"Have you ever done this before?" the instructor asked her.

"Uh huh," she replied, desperately watching the water for a big wave.

"Well, there are a few ground rules that we need to cover first. There's a safe way to ride a wave and an unsafe way. Here at the Ebbtide we try our best to teach every participant the safest way to surf."

Harper was listening to the man's instructions along with the others who had joined their group, but he was watching Alexis. She looked like a dog on a leash, ready to go.

Alexis tightened her grip on the surfboard. She had seen one perfect wave come in, and she knew that the next one would be hers. She'd show Harper Evans a thing or two . . . wouldn't he be surprised? She heard the instructor's voice droning on.

Harper took a step back, trying to make more room for the others who'd joined them as they crowded around the instructors. He bent to put his surfboard down.

Out of the corner of her eye, Alexis saw Harper move, so she shot a quick glance back at the gulf. Sure enough, there was a beautiful wave trying to form. Without another thought, Alexis began to run, tossing her sunglasses back behind her as she went, ignoring the warning voice of her instructor calling after her. She had to beat Harper, and she was afraid he had made plans for this wave, too.

Alexis felt wet globs of sand flick up against her legs as she ran, and the exhilarating sea air urged her on. Finally, she hit the water and began to paddle toward the wave, giving it everything she had. When she was at last standing on the board, riding toward the shore once again, she knew she'd scored a victory. Then the sun caught everything within her view and turned it into one bright, shiny piece of foil.

A voice came to her, a friendly, unfamiliar masculine tone, repeating her name again and again. She wanted to answer, she really did, but her mouth just wouldn't cooperate. Everything was out of sync.

"Miss Cartwright, can you hear me?"

The voice sounded so nice, so friendly.

"Miss Cartwright."

"Mmm," she managed.

"Miss Cartwright, you've had a minor accident. You're in the emergency room of our local hospital, and we've checked you for any possible broken bones or internal problems."

"Mmm." She strained to see whoever was talking. There was a bright light and a figure in front of her. She tried to sit up.

"I've given you some pain medication. You've had a nasty blow to the head, and it's going to be sore for a few days, but other than that, you're fine."

The doctor reached over and helped her sit up. Her blurred vision was clearing, and she saw the doctor and a nurse standing next to her bed. She felt wet and dirty. Gritty sand seemed to be everywhere.

"Your friend is outside waiting for you, and he'll take you back to your hotel. Get a good night's rest, take two of these tablets every four hours for pain, and stay off surfboards for a while."

He smiled at her and she smiled back, wondering who her friend was, but the movement hurt her forehead and she winced, snaking one hand up to the spot where the pain originated.

"Ohhh," she groaned. It had been a mistake to try to touch it.

"The shot I gave you is pretty strong and will take effect very shortly. You shouldn't feel much for the next eight hours at least. My advice is to just get yourself into bed."

"Thank you." She looked forward to it. She felt as if her head might break apart.

The nurse wheeled her out of the emergency room, and Alexis passively sat in the wheelchair, feeling woozy as she was pushed along. Leaning up against the far corridor wall was Harper, scowling at her. The nurse led her to him.

"I've paid your bill. I have a cab waiting," he said briskly, following the nurse who wheeled her down the hall and to the doors. He took her arm as she stood and led her to the cab.

"Why are you here?"

"I drew the shortest straw. I've always been a lucky sort of fellow."

He helped her into the waiting cab, and she began to laugh despite the pain that spread across her forehead every time she exhaled. There were a hundred questions she wanted to ask, but Alexis was too giddy to do anything but laugh. She clapped her hands. "You look a sight."

"Do you want a mirror?"

"Where's your shirt?"

"You've got it on," he replied in the same curt tone he'd used with her ever since he'd met her outside the emergency room.

She looked down at herself for the first time. Seeing Harper barefoot with his hair wildly windblown, his shirt gone, and his wallet stuck in the waistband of his clinging bathing suit had made her want to laugh. But when she saw that she was wearing his shirt, all her questions returned with a rush.

Responding to the astonished look on her face, Harper began to talk. "I was looking forward to the outing this afternoon, intent upon learning something about surfing. Unfortunately, I happened to get stuck in a group that had a woman who thought she knew everything there was to know about the subject."

The taxi driver appeared unconcerned, but Alexis could tell he was listening in on their conversation. Every now and then she could see him look at them in his rearview mirror. It wasn't the driver's fault for being nosy, considering that Harper was talking loudly enough to attract an audience.

"Before anyone with any sense could stop this woman, she ran out and caught a wave that was obvi-

93

ously more than she'd bargained for. The instructor tried to warn her. He even chased after her for a few seconds, but she was racing into the water like there were a hundred demons after her."

As he paused for a breath and a shake of his head, Alexis fingered the wet T-shirt she was wearing. Her mind was still muddled, but almost unconsciously she reached to adjust her bikini strap. Slowly, she moved her fingers across her left collarbone toward her shoulder. Finding nothing, she rubbed again. Then she reached across to the other shoulder and then downward, trying to be inconspicuous but knowing that something was not right.

"Now the woman made it out to the wave all right, but as soon as she stood up on that surfboard, I knew she was in trouble." Harper watched Alexis, never pausing in his story. He observed what she was doing, and a smile broke across his face as he spoke. "The instructor was yelling. I started running, but nobody could help this woman. The last thing I saw was her head hitting her surfboard." He let his eyes meet hers. "You were lucky you didn't drown," he chastised her.

Alexis let her fingers make a quick check, running along the top of her breast and then to her back. Her bikini top was gone. Disappeared.

"Yes, well, I can hardly disagree, can I? I don't remember a thing except standing up on that board, thinking I'd made it." She felt one more time across her back and then moved her hands down into her lap. What on earth had happened? Her head ached.

"You certainly got the attention you were looking

for." Harper raised one eyebrow, pursed his lips, and looked pointedly over at his shirt.

Alexis gasped, looked into the rearview mirror, saw the taxi driver staring back at her, and shot him a glare that made him turn back to his driving. Her face burned with humiliation.

"You're the rudest man I ever met," she whispered scathingly. "Where are the rest of my clothes?" She felt for the bottom of her bathing suit and was rewarded with a sandy, damp strip of cloth.

Toying with her, Harper merely smiled mysteriously for a second. "I don't have your clothes." His voice was loud enough to make the driver turn his head for a quick glance back at them, and when he did, Harper shrugged his shoulders and gave the driver a conspiratorial wink.

Like a bolt out of the blue, Alexis felt a curtain go down around her mind and her body ease into a state of complete relaxation. The pain medication was taking effect, she thought, but she made herself speak. "You know what I'm talking about, Mr. Evans."

"Do you want to hear the ending to my story?" he asked dryly, seeing that they were almost at the hotel.

Alexis didn't know if she could hold her head up any longer. Suddenly, it felt so very heavy.

"Well, do you or don't you?"

"You're going to tell it, anyway, aren't you?" She closed her eyes. Finding out what had happened didn't seem quite as important right now as it had a few minutes earlier. Right now she only wanted to get into bed.

"The instructor and another helpful person who shall remain nameless swam out and pulled you back in. When we got you to shore, it seemed you needed a little covering up. It wouldn't do to have you lying out there semi-clothed, now would it?"

She raised one hand, wanting to shout, but finding no strength. "I . . . oh, never mind." She couldn't think.

"Then somebody had to go with you in the ambulance, and I decided it was in my best interests to look after my shirt. It goes with my bathing suit, you know."

She knew he was mocking her, but she was fading fast. She'd never taken medication well. Two aspirin would have been enough, she thought. She should have told that doctor, but it was too late. Her head was swimming.

The cab pulled up in front of the hotel.

"Drive us around to the back, will you? I may have some trouble getting her upstairs." Harper saw the way Alexis was slumped against the seat, her head twisting slowly forward. The nurse was right. She'd told him that Alexis would be practically unconscious by the time he got her back to the hotel.

Harper helped her out of the cab and got her into the kitchen. He ordered a cup of hot tea to be sent to her room as he walked by the cooks, shrugging away their offers of help. But by the time he got her up to her room, he wished he'd said yes to them. As light as she was, he had a hard time leaning her against something while he got her into the elevator.

Riding up to the sixth floor, it dawned on Harper that he couldn't take her to her room. He didn't have a key. She was leaning her head against his shoulder, hardly aware of where she was, and he kept his arm wrapped around her so that she wouldn't fall.

"I never should have gotten involved," he whispered, cursing himself. She was bringing out all the wrong kinds of emotions in him. Carefully, he tightened his arm protectively around her smooth, soft shoulder and gritted his teeth.

CHAPTER FIVE

There was nothing else to do. When Harper stepped out of the elevator, he turned left and guided her to his room. He could hardly leave her slumped up against her hotel door while he ran to get a key. It would be easier this way, he told himself, trying to ignore a nagging doubt. Was that the real reason?

"I'm going to call up Miss Sally, and I'll have the hotel manager bring up a key to your room, Alexis. Right now, let's just get you in here." He was grateful that the hotel manager had sent over his wallet and keys when he'd called for them from the hospital.

"Miss Sally? Do we want her?" Groggy from the medication, Alexis felt almost like a child again. Dimly, she was aware of where she was and what she was doing, but none of it bothered her much, and now her head didn't hurt at all. It just felt numb.

"I have to tell her you won't be able to meet her for dinner." Harper helped her in and sat her down on the edge of his kingsize bed.

"No, I don't think I will," Alexis said, and fell back on the bed. "I think I'll just rest here a minute." She closed her eyes.

"God, how right I was. I never should have gotten involved," Harper said softly. He looked down at her, aware of the sand and grit that clung to her body, knowing she shouldn't be allowed to sleep that way. He watched the way her eyes were closed shut, the faint blue veins of her eyelids looking a little like delicate spiderwebs. Her breathing had become light and steady. He listened.

After a few seconds he turned to the phone and called Miss Sally, assuring the woman that Alexis would be all right and asking that Alexis's room be unlocked. He glanced down at the sleeping figure. He didn't know quite what he was going to do with her now.

"Alexis," he called, hating to disturb her. "Alexis, wake up. I'll take you to your room."

"Just give me a minute more here." Her voice floated faintly up from the bedspread. She turned over on her side and curled her body up, never opening her eyes.

What difference would a few minutes make? Harper asked himself. He walked over to the bay window and looked out at the night. Thinking he'd heard her move, he glanced quickly over at the bed and then back to the view outside his window. He sighed. He wished he hadn't given up cigarettes. Right now he needed one.

After a while he went back to the edge of the bed and leaned over. "Alexis, we need to get you out of those wet clothes and into your bed."

Her eyelids fluttered and opened. "That's a good idea," she said, but her words sounded like one long slur. She smiled a vague smile, her eyes glassy.

"Hang on to me," Harper demanded, pulling her up and adjusting her body against his own so that he could walk with her. She still felt damp to the touch, and her hair fell in downy ringlets all around her head. He sucked in his breath. All he wanted was to get this over with.

When Harper turned the doorknob of Alexis's room, he was relieved that it opened. Then he saw that he shouldn't have worried about the hotel staff taking care of things. Two vases of fresh flowers had been placed on the dresser and on one side table. Alexis's bed had been carefully turned down. Muted light shone from the nearby table lamp, and on a silver tray was the hot tea he'd requested, as well as the bottle of bourbon, soda, and ice which he'd asked for as an afterthought.

"Let's start your shower." He kicked the door shut.

"Uh huh." Alexis tried to say something, but her mind was too foggy.

Hearing the way she yielded to his suggestion, and looking at her clouded eyes, Harper knew she shouldn't be left alone. The fact that she didn't answer told him the woman was too far gone to take care of herself.

She held onto the bathroom doorframe and stared vacantly into his brown eyes. She opened her mouth and then softly closed it, forgetting what it was she'd intended to say.

Harper put his arm around her, afraid to leave her for too long without his support. Taking her with him, he went to the side of the old tub and turned on the shower faucets, then waited a few seconds so that he could adjust the water temperature.

While he waited, he began to help her out of her

clothes, immediately realizing that she wasn't going to be able to do it herself. When he began to move the damp T-shirt upward, its weight made it cling to her like paste, and he made a conscious effort to be gentle with her. Alexis made no move to resist but remained passively still, practically limp weight in his arms.

His mind racing and his fingers slightly trembling, Harper ran his hand along the waistband of her wet bathing suit and pulled it off. With a supreme act of willpower, he forced himself to be clinical in his ministrations.

Right now Alexis was at her most vulnerable, a woman in need of care, and the feelings inside him said he wanted to respond to her, care for her in a manner far different from the way he'd behaved with her before. After he'd showered her off, letting the spray wash away most of the sand, Harper dried her with the largest towel he could find. His hands shook as he worked with hasty, unplanned movements. Being with her like this was more than a man could stand, and he heard his own breath coming in low, raspy gulps.

"Dammit all, Alexis. You've got me talking to myself now. This isn't fair."

She clung to him with eyes nearly closed, more like a rag doll than the vibrant woman he'd come to know. The bump on her head was swelling, and he told himself he'd need to use compresses on it to help keep the swelling down, but that would have to come later.

It wasn't until he'd finished with his attempt at drying her off that he began to look around for a gown. There was nothing in the bathroom, and so he took another dry towel and wrapped it around her, tucking the ends together so that they held the towel closed. His hand brushed against her warm breast, and his face flushed bright red. He felt like an awkward schoolboy. She didn't weigh much, but she was becoming heavier and heavier each time she settled her body against his.

Already the towel was coming loose from where he'd clasped it together, revealing the swell of her breasts as they rose and fell in a steady rhythm. He could smell the dampness of her skin and was uncomfortably aware of the way his body was reacting to her nearness.

"Hell and damnation, Alexis. What am I doing?" He wrapped one of her arms around his neck and led her toward the turned-down bed.

The towel began to slide downward, and it fell completely off her when they had almost gotten to the bed. He was grateful she didn't know what was happening. If she could see herself now, there was no telling what would happen. Without ceremony, he placed her on the bed and lay her back against the pillow before lifting her legs up and quickly tucking her under the fresh sheets.

Alexis was only aware of vague sensations and couldn't comprehend what was happening. She knew she'd been in the shower, and now Harper was here and she was in a bed. Giving in to the darkness that was consuming her, Alexis felt the touch of a hand against her cheek.

Harper took his hand away. She didn't seem to have any fever, but he'd never seen anyone respond to medication so strongly. Her eyes were closed, and she lay very still where he'd placed her.

Rummaging through the dresser, he found a gown for her, but when he went back to where she was, he decided not to try to put it on her. She wouldn't even notice she wasn't wearing a gown. Not until tomorrow, at least. Right now she was sound asleep, off in some far away place of her own.

He put the gown down and walked over to the bottle of bourbon. Deciding a drink was in order, he poured a little of the liquor in a glass, added a splash of soda, and downed it with one urgent gulp. Harper felt the jolt of the alcohol going down his throat, and it was then that he realized he was sweating. A fine film of perspiration coated his face.

Not satisfied that she was going to be all right, and trying to submerge the desire he felt so strongly, Harper went back into the bathroom and made a compress. Then he went to sit on the edge of the bed and applied the cloth to Alexis's forehead. He tried his best to be gentle with her. He didn't want to disturb her, not now when she looked so peaceful and relaxed.

Later he crawled onto the bed beside her, making sure to sleep on top of the sheet so that their bodies would not touch. She'd have a fit, he knew, but someone had to look after her, and it seemed he was the appointed one.

Listening to her soft breathing, Harper felt his body begin to relax. Once, before he fell asleep, he heard a moan from her side of the bed, and he moved his pillow so that his face would be close to her during the night in case she needed him.

Alexis awoke with a throbbing headache and patchy memories. Patterned sunlight shone through the partially opened drapes; enough so that she could see a towel on the floor and her blue gown at the foot of her bed.

If her gown was on the bed . . . ? Hastily, she peered under the covers. How in the world had she ended up like this?

"Oh, my God," she yelled when she saw Harper watching her from the other side of the bed. "What happened?" Flustered, Alexis held the sheet up to her throat and at the same time reached for her aching head.

Harper rolled over on his back. "How do you feel?"

"Crazy. That's how I feel. What are you doing here?"

"How much do you remember about last night?"

She looked around the room. "Evidently not enough. You brought me to my room. I remember that much. After that it's all a blur." She leaned back against the pillow. "So you tell me, but first . . ." She stopped in mid-sentence. "Tell me why you slept in my bed."

"Because you needed someone to look after you. That medication you took really knocked you out." He was pleased at the way she was responding to all this. He hadn't expected her to be quite so rational.

"How did I . . . ?"

Again she didn't finish, but he could tell what she was thinking. "I helped you with your shower, but you were so out of it, I didn't think you'd miss your

104

gown. Besides, it would have taken me forever to put it on you." He grinned.

Her cheeks reddened, but she didn't look away from him. "I don't know whether to slap you or thank you."

He couldn't restrain his laughter. "You'd better thank me. I'm the only person you had to rely on yesterday, and I acted the perfect gentleman."

The memories of her accident and the ride home in the cab with Harper gradually returned, and she knew he was right. She did need to thank him, but the sight of him lying so near to her filled her with so many conflicting emotions, she could hardly think straight. His hair was tousled, and his sleepy face looked soft and gentle. The hard, cynical man of the last few days had disappeared, replaced by an extremely sensual man whose very presence here suggested sensitivity and concern.

She felt her forehead again. "This bump on my head is no bump. It's the size of an ostrich egg."

Rolling over on his side, Harper propped his head on his hand and studied her for a second. "Or that of a large goose," he teased.

"I must look a disaster," Alexis moaned, self-consciously running her fingers through her hair.

"I probably shouldn't give your ego such a boost, but you look good." His gaze ran from her face, down to where she'd carelessly let the sheet fall below her neck. He held it there.

She thought maybe it was the huskiness of his voice or the tantalizing way he was looking at her. Whatever it was, Alexis was once again aware of the sexual tension that always seemed to exist between the two of them. It was like a living thing, a liquid fire that refused to be extinguished.

She tried to ignore it. "What can I do to thank you, Harper? I can take care of myself now."

"Well, at least we agree on something."

This time she refused to raise her eyes to his. Lightly, she asked, "What's that?"

"You owe me something for what I've done for you." A rush of feelings assailed him. A conflict like he'd never known was going on inside him. Seeing her there, all soft and lovely, after all they'd been through together for the last few days, made him aware of how much he wanted this woman, but at the same time he knew he shouldn't. How could he fight it? he wondered.

"You're right."

"I've helped you out. Right?"

"Yes."

"Then I want a favor from you."

She ran her fingers along her bottom lip in hesitation. "What is it?"

"I'm not leaving your bed until you tell me why you behaved the way you did, Alexis. I want to know why you took advantage of me. You owe me that much."

Nervously, she gripped the sheet. The serious tone of his voice disturbed her. "Can't we wait a little while, Harper? I don't think this is the place to discuss this." She brushed her fingers across her forehead and winced.

Harper got up, went into the bathroom, and returned with a pill in one hand and a glass of water in the other. He sat on the edge of the bed, gave her the

106

glass and the pill, then placed one arm on one side of her and his other arm on the edge of the pillow, hemming her in. "That night out on the beach, why didn't you say anything to me about your purpose here? Why did you let me think you were just a tourist?"

"I—"

"Take your pill," he demanded, waiting while she took it, then putting his arms in front of her again.

"You duped me, Alexis!" His dark brown eyes caught and held hers.

He sat close, with his shoulders hunched forward, and Alexis felt trapped.

"Give me . . . give me a chance to explain, Harper," she tried.

"Explain?" He bit off each syllable. "What makes you think you can explain what you did? Dammit, you played me for a fool. A total fool."

"Nooo," she moaned. "That's not true."

"Then what was it? I want to know." He sucked down hard on his lower lip. He wasn't fighting fair, he knew, but the woman was eating him alive. The events of the last few days had pushed him beyond the point of logic.

Alexis felt her throat burn. "Harper." She swallowed and shut her eyes. She could feel his intense gaze burning through her, his face one dark cloud.

"It was a mistake. At first it was just a hunch. I didn't know you were here to buy the Ebbtide. Not for sure."

"That's comforting," he said dryly, his impatience simmering just below the surface. "But not good enough."

"It's true," she murmured, leaning her head against the pillow. What was the use?

"Go on."

"No," she stated firmly, raising her head to face him. "Not until you agree to give me the courtesy of listening."

A grin started at the corners of his mouth and spread. "I wish you could see yourself."

"Why?"

"You look like one of Napoleon's troops, ready to go to battle one last time."

"Are you ready to listen? I'm losing interest fast, Harper."

"Try me." He watched her face, wondering for the hundredth time how he'd let himself end up like this. The memory of her smooth flesh sent a shiver through him, and he squeezed his eyes shut, trying to blank it out.

"I apologize. That's something I guess I don't do very often, but I see how much I've hurt you and I'm sorry. I never intended it. At first I was trying to be loyal to Miss Sally and her request for secrecy."

"You haven't hurt me. Angered me, yes. Hurt me, no," he insisted, moving his arms closer to her.

"Okay. I don't feel like getting into a discussion on semantics right now." She lifted up her hand in a gesture designed to end their argument before it could begin. "Yes, I had a suspicion about you, especially when I thought about what you'd said about your work, and after you told me about your wife's ending up with the vacation spot."

"Go on." He was still staring at her, but the intensity in his eyes had changed.

"Don't you see? By the time I really, really began to suspect that you and I were here for the same reason, I didn't want it to be."

"You didn't?"

It was too late for pretense, and she had no energy for subterfuge. "I was enjoying being with you. I didn't want it to be true."

"Do you expect me to believe that?"

A quick flash of fury shot into her eyes. "Does it really matter to you?" She eased over on her side, forgetting about her head. "Ohhh," she screamed.

He reached for her, and when he did, he felt a painful thrust of desire. "Be careful," he said gravely.

"See what you made me do?" she complained, feeling bold jabs of pain from where she'd jammed her head into the pillow.

"See what you made me do?" he whispered, cradling her into his arms. After the briefest of moments had passed, Harper drew her face to his, moving her chin slowly toward him.

His tone sent a strangely pleasant sensation throughout her body. She was totally unprepared for his kiss, but her mouth opened willingly, and she felt herself responding to his probing tongue. It was as if a jolt of electric current were rushing through her body as his warm mouth took possession of hers.

Harper ran one hand down along her back and then upward, until he held her head in his powerful grip. His tongue made a thorough investigation of the recesses of her mouth, stopping, moving, exploring gently at first and then with more intensity until she felt all her resistance melt away. Soon she was meeting his kiss with her own.

She let her mouth work smoothly with his, caught up in the languid spell Harper had so easily cast over her. Pulling one hand out from under the sheet, she reached out and touched his muscular arm and shoulders. Finally, her fingers tangled in his thick, dark hair.

Lost in the thrill of her touch, Harper found all his initial reactions rekindled as he remembered the beauty of her first kiss, and the vibrant response he was discovering in her now. She was like no other woman he'd ever been with.

Alexis opened her eyes and felt him pull his mouth away from her, still holding her to him. Through a mellowed haze, Alexis cautioned herself. It would be difficult to resist any more advances of this man who seemed to know just what to say and do.

Harper raked his thumb along her lower lip, caught up in the thrill of holding her. Then his mouth once again began its assault on hers, pushing his tongue between her lips until it sank softly into the moist, warm cavern of her mouth. Finesse was forgotten as Alexis responded, matching the force of his kiss with her own surge of passion. He brought his hands around to stroke her arms and then her throat, resting at last in the wet tangle of lively red curls.

She clasped either side of his face and fought to clear her head of the effects of the medication, wanting only to enjoy the pleasure she'd just begun to discover. She felt his tongue move along the ridge of her teeth, and she pushed her tongue brazenly against his.

For a moment, he grasped it with his lips, tugging,

110

teasing, making her powerless to even think of resisting. When he abandoned her mouth to explore the softness between the rise of her cleavage, she had a split second to think before his mouth moved upward to command hers again.

It wouldn't ever work out. She knew. Business and pleasure never did, and their beliefs were totally opposed to one another's, but the very human part of her wouldn't deny how much she thrilled to his demanding, sensual embrace, and she wanted to enjoy it, if only for the moment.

His firm mouth gently swooped down to tease her delicate lips, taking advantage of her slow response to enter the inner softness of her mouth again and continue his slow discovery. His hand moved slowly beneath the sheet to caress the softness of her naked breast.

He felt like a drowning man. "How can this happen? We don't even like each other," he exclaimed, forcing himself to pull away from her.

"I know." Her head felt heavy, and she brought it down to lean against his chest.

He could feel the butterfly touch of her eyelashes against his flesh, and the utter delicateness of her cheek. He brought his hand up to caress her face, pushing aside the sheet that separated them. He moved her back against the pillow, and his lips began to skim lightly down her throat to her firm breasts.

Gradually, he slipped the cotton sheet lower and lower so that her entire upper body was exposed to his roaming hands and fiery caress. With warm, agile fingers, Harper traced a faint line from her throat, down and under her breasts, creating a hard surge of tension in each one.

"Harper, we can't do this." Almost lost in the pleasure of his touch, Alexis felt her resistance disappear. As she listened to his heartbeat, a strong, wild pumping, she blocked everything else out of her mind.

At the door came a loud knock followed by two more. "Room service, Miss Cartwright. Miss Sally said you might need a good breakfast."

Grinding his teeth in frustration, Harper straightened his shoulders and pulled the sheet back up to her throat. "I guess you could say you were saved by the bell," he muttered. He took one last look at her and opened the door, leaving before she could reply.

CHAPTER SIX

After eating the breakfast Miss Sally had sent, Alexis went back to sleep. Much later, she opened her eyes and looked around the room. Her body felt as though she'd been used as a battering ram. Every time she moved, she felt something new hurt.

Alexis got up slowly and went to search through the bathroom for the pain pills the doctor had given her. Her head felt enormous, and the entire side of her face hurt. Finding the pills on the counter, she read the directions and then took two before looking into the mirror.

"If possible, Alexis Bain Cartwright, you look even worse than you did last night," she said to her reflection.

She turned on the water, let it run until steam rose up, and then, using a clean washrag and the hot water, made a compress to apply to the painful bump on her head. Restlessly, she walked around the hotel room.

Outside, the sun shone brightly. It would be another beautiful day, she was sure, yet the thought did nothing to cheer her.

The compress cooled, and she went back to the bathroom and applied more hot water, then returned to the bay window, waiting for the medication to take effect. She opened the window and looked down at the scene below.

Since the moment she'd awakened, Alexis had tried not to think about Harper and all that had taken place between them. The mere thought of him accentuated the regret she already felt. Now, as she looked down, she saw him standing outside the hotel, gazing critically back toward the front veranda, blueprints in his hand.

She pulled her head back in and closed the window. Her pulse raced as an unexpected feeling of anxiety washed over her, and she traced a wayward finger across her lips.

Despite his thoughtfulness and the gentle way he'd taken care of her, Alexis knew that she must forget what had happened between them. Seeing him outside the hotel was a jarringly rude reminder of their differences.

She began to worry that she had gotten herself into an impossible situation. She absolutely couldn't let herself succumb to Harper's charming ways. They had no future together, and a three- or four-day interlude held no appeal.

Alexis paced slowly back to the bed and got in. She pulled the covers up to her chin and thanked the medication as she felt a foggy haze return. "Just in time," she mumbled before falling back to sleep.

The shrill ring of the telephone broke through to her sometime later. She opened her eyes, instantly aware of feeling much better.

"Hello."

"Miss Cartwright—Alexis, how are you?" Miss

Sally's voice sang. "I was planning to call you earlier, but I decided I'd let you rest as long as possible."

"That was very thoughtful of you." Sitting up, Alexis tried to guess the time. She felt as if she'd slept another hour or two.

"Tell me, dear, how are you feeling?"

"Actually, I feel much better," Alexis was happy to report. Her head still hurt but nothing like before.

"Good. I've been worried about you. I was wondering, Alexis, if you're really feeling better, would you like to take a look at our accounts this afternoon and perhaps take one more tour of the hotel?"

"Well, I—"

"Mr. Evans and Mr. Carson have requested it. They'll be coming to my apartment in about an hour. We'll start with a look at the Ebbtide books. What do you say?"

How could she refuse? "I'll be there."

"Good. See you then."

Hanging up the telephone, Alexis had to wonder who'd initiated the afternoon meeting, and then she cautioned herself to be on guard. She was dealing with two men who wanted the same thing she did, and the competition would soon begin to heighten between the three of them.

She knew how Harper felt. He'd let her know he intended to own the Ebbtide, come what may. As for Mr. Carson, she still hadn't figured him out, but there was something about him that bothered her. She couldn't quite put her finger on it, but it was unquestionably there, like a late-afternoon shadow.

Calling room service, Alexis asked the time and

found it was already one o'clock. She'd slept over sixteen hours. No wonder she felt better.

The telephone rang again just as she finished her shower. "Hello," she began a little breathlessly.

"Alexis, I'm sorry to bother you again, dear, but something important has come up. I won't be able to make our little meeting," Miss Sally said apologetically.

"Oh, that's all right."

"I was wondering if you could have dinner with me this evening. Mr. Evans and Mr. Carson have agreed to come, and if you say yes, we'll have our little group all together again. Yesterday was sort of a lost day for all of us," she added.

"Yes," Alexis said, laughing, tenderly touching her head. "I know what you mean."

"It seems Mr. Evans has business elsewhere he must attend to, and he's asked that the bidding be moved up to Friday. Would you mind, dear?"

Her mind racing with the implications of Harper's request, Alexis stalled for a moment. Was it just a ploy to gain some advantage in the bidding, or did he merely want to get away from her?

"I wouldn't mind at all, Miss Sally. I need to get back to Houston, myself." She hung up then, trying to think things through.

Alexis knew it would be to her disadvantage not to have dinner with the group, but she wished she could come up with some plausible excuse to avoid it. The thought of being around Harper was disturbing enough right now, and she didn't want to see him any more than she had to.

Something had happened between them early this

morning. Something had sprung to life that she hadn't been aware of before, but it had obviously affected only her. There was no point in her trying to deal with it all now, she knew. She only wanted to ignore the thoughts that were bombarding her, threatening her peace of mind. If she let them rise to the surface and out into the open, she'd be lost. She wondered if she wasn't already.

By the time she arrived at Miss Ferguson's door, the men were already seated. The apartment door had been left slightly ajar, and Alexis caught sight of Harper, his expression businesslike and serious as he sat with his head down, looking through a small pile of typewritten papers.

A curious feeling gripped her for an instant. She felt something for Harper, something more than mere physical attraction. A shudder ran through her, and she did her best to forget what she had just come to understand. This man was her adversary, no matter what kind of feelings she'd developed for him. He knew it and she'd better not let herself forget it, either.

Miss Sally greeted her warmly. "Good afternoon, Miss Cartwright."

Alexis entered an airy living room filled with antiques and beautiful furniture. This is the part of the hotel I'll keep for myself, she silently promised.

"Miss Cartwright." Mr. Carson nodded, standing up as she entered.

"How do you feel?" Harper asked solicitously.

"Much better, thank you."

Harper watched her while their hostess asked about Alexis's accident. He was trying very hard to

117

ignore the emotional responses she invoked in him, but he knew he stood no chance of winning.

"How's your head? Are you taking your pills?"

"It still hurts." She smiled up at him. "I decided to forego the pills. I took two aspirins instead."

"Why?"

"I didn't particularly like the way they affected me." She felt his searching gaze on her, and she turned away. Let him think what he would.

"Now, then," Miss Sally was saying, "let's have a look at the accounts. These sheets will give you a brief summary of our debits and credits for the past year. Those black books on the table cover the past five years." She waited. "I'm going to pour all of us some coffee while you take a look. My financial statement is right there."

"Here's something you might be interested in. An itemized list of repairs done to the building since January of last year," Harper told Alexis, handing her a folder.

Now that he knew she was all right he was angry again. He'd made a vow to himself that he'd keep his cool, but he was already losing it. Since six-thirty in the morning he'd paced around the Ebbtide, calculating the renovation costs, telling himself it was vital to prove his point.

Here was Alexis standing there across the coffee table from him, cool as a cucumber, confidently planning to save this monstrosity. She was looking all around the room with adoring eyes, and Harper knew the whole damned thing was useless. He shouldn't even bother trying to show her the error of her ways.

Alexis sat down on the peach Chippendale sofa next to Mr. Carson. Harper was sitting in a high wing chair, using his attaché case as a lap desk.

"Thank you." She nodded, trying to ignore the tension which once again stood between them. She could feel Mr. Carson's eyes on her and she turned to him.

"You're the only one without an attaché case," he commented. "Do you have one?"

"She doesn't need any information, Mr. Carson. If you've got more than enough money to throw away, you don't need reports or attaché cases for carrying around information you won't bother to use."

The air felt heavy and thick. Stunned, Alexis said nothing, but she was furious—at herself as much as Harper. She should never have bothered feeling grateful to him. He obviously hadn't acted out of any sense of concern for her.

Their eyes met and locked, sending first one message and then another. Alexis's face began to burn with the memory of his touch. How could she have let herself think for even an instant that she was feeling something tender and meaningful for this antagonistic man?

"I keep almost all of my important papers in my attaché case, Mr. Carson." She lifted her chin and turned from Harper, ignoring his belligerent expression. "Today, though, I brought only my notebook." She reached inside her purse and pulled it out. "I keep all the information I need in here."

"Coffee?" Miss Sally served her, then Mr. Carson, and finally Harper.

Alexis looked through the expense sheets Harper

had thrust into her hand earlier, still wondering at Mr. Carson's unusual question. One look at the expense sheets said they were about as bad as she'd expected. The thing Harper didn't seem to understand was that once extensive renovation had been done, these kinds of repairs would become unnecessary.

After another thirty minutes had passed, Alexis pushed aside the folders she'd been perusing and stood up. Miss Sally was standing in her kitchen, so Alexis took her empty coffee cup and went to talk to her.

"I knew you all didn't need me, so I turned on my television. *General Hospital* comes on now, you see, and I'm afraid I've become quite addicted to it." The older woman took the cup and saucer from Alexis and rinsed them out, then set them in the sink.

"I see." Alexis grinned, taking in the charm of the modern yellow-and-white galley kitchen.

"Are you all ready for your tour?"

"We can wait until your program's over. I don't know if the others are ready or not."

"No, indeed." Miss Sally winked. "I can watch this tomorrow. Let me ask Mr. Carson and Mr. Evans if they're ready."

After everyone agreed to put the books aside, they rode the elevator to the top of the building.

"You know, Miss Sally, I've been thinking," Alexis said as they were getting out. "This hotel might be worth a historical marker. The Ionic columns in front of the building are among the most richly detailed I've ever seen, and I'm convinced there are

120

many features of the hotel that are absolutely unique."

Miss Sally agreed while the others examined the roof, which was badly in need of repair. Alexis stood in silence, also noting the condition of the roof, and looking out over the most spectacular view of the gulf she'd ever seen. A little fresh air might help her regain her perspective, she hoped, because being around Harper somehow wreaked havoc with her ability to think clearly.

Harper walked over to her. "If miracles occurred and you were the one who got the Ebbtide, do you have any idea what you're going to have to charge to get your money back out of this place? Or do you even intend to try?"

She stiffened and swung around to face him. "Is that all you can think about?"

"I'm trying to show you something, make you understand," he said with exaggerated patience.

"Understand? I think I understand, all right. You want to show me I'm wrong, not because you care about me but because you're a bully. You think you can berate and browbeat me until I give up and agree with you." She shook her head. "Well, thanks but no thanks. I know what I'm doing."

He watched the sunlight beam down on her crown of majestic red hair. Every now and then when she moved her head a certain way, he could see the huge bump, and it reminded him of the night before and how he'd held her in his arms in the early-morning hours. That moment seemed a long time in the past.

Harper grimaced. "If I could believe you knew

what you were doing, even against my better judgment I would force myself to leave you alone."

"While we're on the subject, I want to remind you of one thing." She looked for the others, but they were standing far away.

"I'm listening," he taunted.

"I am not using my father's money for this, Harper. I'm using my own," she said, her voice full of indignation.

"If I believed that, I'd be even more insistent that you listen to reason." He stepped toward her. "It's a foolish waste."

"So far you've managed to call me a liar and a fool, almost in one breath." She fought back tears. "Well, frankly, I don't care what you think."

"How much is all this going to cost? This renovation? And how much would you then have to charge for a room?" he shot back.

"I don't know yet."

"Of course you don't."

"Oh, come now. Can you tell me how much you're planning to spend?"

"Practically to the penny."

"Now it's my turn for disbelief."

"Are you two ready to go down to the basement?" Mr. Carson was approaching the elevator. Miss Sally motioned for Alexis and Harper to join them.

Alexis was determined not to give up, no matter how uncomfortable it made the others. She was blackly furious, ready to fight, create a scene, do anything to make him listen to her.

When the elevator had started down, she said to Harper, "I don't suppose you've ever considered the thought that there are many people in this world who would be happy, maybe eager, to pay a little more for something that has a certain ambiance, a sense of style, and an extra touch of elegance."

"Nobody's crazy enough to pay a fortune for a night in an old wreck of a hotel."

She looked at the others and smiled at Harper sarcastically. She swore she wouldn't let anyone know how he truly affected her. "You seem to have a gift for exaggeration, Harper. I wasn't thinking about spending a fortune. Only a few dollars more. Only enough to take the bid away from you."

They stepped out of the elevator, and Miss Sally looked at Mr. Carson. "Doesn't take much to guess what these two are fighting about. What are your plans for the Ebbtide? If you're the lucky buyer, I mean."

Mr. Carson looked away. "I'm not sure yet," he answered evasively.

There was an uncomfortable period of silence then. The man absolutely gave Alexis the willies. She didn't understand why she felt the way she did, but she doubted that Mr. Carson could be trusted. She wished she could discuss it with Harper, but that was an impossibility. She and Harper were once again like prizefighters, squared off against one another.

"The water heating system is a bit antiquated." Miss Sally laughed, as if trying to dispel the tension that had settled on the little group. "Years ago people didn't take as many baths as they do now."

Harper's voice rang out, joining hers in the dark underground room. He stepped past Alexis toward the massive boilers.

As he passed, he whispered to her, "So that's why you were trembling last night. For a while there I thought there might have been another reason."

It was a first. The first time he'd referred to what had happened between them and now it was up to Alexis to try to decipher his meaning. She couldn't be certain if he was merely tormenting her with a reminder of their intimate moments or if he was letting her know that she'd affected him.

"This is a part of our sprinkler system. You've probably noticed them throughout the building." Pointing to the ceiling, Miss Sally showed them the basement sprinkler heads.

"Miss Ferguson, I'd like to know the recharge time on your boiler system, and then if you'll show me the electrical system, I must be going. I have another appointment soon," Mr. Carson said with a vague hint of impatience in his voice.

"Take all the time you want," Miss Sally said to Alexis and Harper.

Watching her take Mr. Carson by the arm and head across the room, Alexis was tempted to join them, but Harper stopped her.

"Look here. You think I'm exaggerating, but I'm serious. This building is beyond salvage." Harper had his pocketknife out and was chipping away at a rust line that ran along one of the sprinkler heads.

With strong, swift moves he scraped away flecks of rust and metal. Alexis watched as he quickly folded up the knife and put it back into his hip pocket before straightening his jacket. She observed his masculine gestures, thinking that there was a certain dignity, a very definite style in the way he did things.

"Are you listening to me?"

"I shouldn't be, but I am." She shifted her eyes from his body to his face. "It's the same old story over and over again."

"You know from the first time I met you I thought you were a smart woman—"

"Don't finish your statement."

"No, now hear me out," he demanded, reaching out and grabbing her arm as she started away.

"Why should I?"

"Okay, maybe I deserved that, but just listen."

"What else can I do, since you're holding me here?" She looked down, feeling the strength of his large hand gripping her arm. Her flesh burned, not so much from the pressure of his touch, but from the reaction occurring inside her.

"Sorry." He dropped his hand to his side. "Alexis, everything in this hotel is so antiquated that even fairly new equipment doesn't work right."

She caught the frustration in his voice. He was intent on hammering his point home.

"I'm sure the sprinkler system doesn't work, and it's only ten or twelve years old," he continued.

"Now, how could you know that?"

"I know," he answered cockily. "Early this morning when I ran through my own personal inspection, I checked the basement system and found that it was inoperable."

Alexis hardly noticed when Miss Sally and Mr. Carson excused themselves. It seemed she and Harper were the last ones to leave a place on their group tours, but she'd rather be with Harper fighting over the hotel than near Mr. Carson. Something about him just made her uneasy.

"In case you haven't noticed, our tour is over."

"You need to see what I'm trying to demonstrate for you first. Then you can go." He was still working with the sprinkler system controls.

"I don't think you understand. I'm not interested in having you prove your point. I don't intend to cooperate." She pursed her lips, feeling anger surge through her. The damned man just wouldn't give up.

"Look here," Harper insisted.

"No, you look here," Alexis retorted. "I'm starving, and I want to leave. I've got to get ready for our next command performance. I promised Miss Sally."

"Look, damn it, just a second." Exasperated, he grabbed for the switch to the sprinkler system. "This thing wouldn't come on if we had a blazing fire going in here. We'd be dead first."

He was fumbling with the control switch. "Stop it," Alexis screamed.

In a flash, water was spraying down on the two of them, soaking them completely within seconds. Harper looked at the control box in amazement and then at Alexis. Her mouth was opened wide in disbelief.

"Ohhhh," she wailed, lifting her hand above her head in a useless gesture. Drenched to the skin, she bit her tongue, trying to hold back the steaming expletives she wanted to shout at Harper. "You . . ." she started, giving in to her emotions. "Damn it all, Harper! You did this on purpose!"

Harper recovered from his surprise and began laughing, a full, deep laugh that welled up from far down inside him. Alexis looked so ridiculous, yet so appealing drenched to the skin, her red curls plastered to her head and her dress clinging to her shapely body, that he couldn't control himself.

Still laughing, he lifted his head toward the ceiling, reveling in the torrent of water, knowing it wouldn't hurt the basement much. He had turned on the water by accident; nevertheless, he found he was thoroughly enjoying the zany episode.

Quivering from anger and the chill that permeated her body, Alexis stormed toward the door. Thinking of a hundred mean, spiteful things she could do for revenge, she stared balefully at Harper. It was too much! He was doubled over, laughing louder than ever.

She began to shout. "One thing about it, you were wrong. The sprinkler system worked." She lowered her voice until she was talking to herself. "But, then, you actually knew it all along."

Before she could slam the door behind her, Alexis heard Harper's voice, his laughter barely subsiding.

"It was worth it. Believe me, seeing you like you are now was worth being wrong. You look just like a waterlogged cat."

CHAPTER SEVEN

Arranging for the basement cleanup was a minor effort on Harper's part. He generously tipped the employees who came with mops and a vacuum pump, staying with them until their job was completed. It had taken a long time for him to recover from his laughing jag, and whenever he thought for too long about Alexis and how she'd looked when the water began pouring down on top of them, he'd burst out in laughter all over again. She'd probably never believe that he hadn't purposely started that sprinkler system.

Returning to his room to change clothes, Harper couldn't get her off his mind. When the elevator stopped on the sixth floor, he got off and headed toward his room feeling cold and uncomfortable in his wet clothes. Halfway there he stopped. He had never intended to douse the two of them with water; it had been just as much of a shock to him as it had been to Alexis. Yet something was still bothering him.

Abruptly, he turned and started back down the hallway in the other direction, his shoes squeaking as he walked. He knocked on the door to Alexis's room.

"Yes, who is it?"

The sound of her voice told him the answer to his

question. As disillusioned as he'd been by her, as deeply as he'd mistrusted her, he couldn't get her out of his system. As hard as he'd tried, it hadn't worked. Things had only worsened.

"It's Harper."

"I'll be down in a few minutes," she called through the closed door.

"I just want to talk to you for a second."

He leaned against the doorjamb as she unlocked the door.

"If you have a water hose with you, I give you fair warning—I'm prepared to strike back this time."

Her hair was still wet, but the ringlets were curled softly all around her head. She had on a silky blue robe, tied at the waist with a full collar that was opened at the neck. The fabric clung to her, catching at the peak of her breasts and cupping under them.

Harper's breath quickened. He wanted to step inside with her, but he only smiled. She was beautiful, this woman with the quicksilver temper and eyes that could melt stone.

"I have nothing in my hand." He shrugged his shoulders and turned his hands over palm upward.

Alexis felt at a loss for what to do or say. As much as she tried to hate him, she just couldn't. He was a tremendously attractive man, even when he was soaking wet, she had to admit. Her heart began pounding in her ears as she reacted to the lazy look of sensuality in his striking face and eyes.

"I'm getting dressed right now. What is it?" She made her voice sound tough and hard. She had to.

Harper sighed, taking his time, trying to decide

what to say. "I'm sorry about your dress. I hope it wasn't ruined."

His voice was like a caress, but she couldn't let herself respond to him as she wanted. "Not if we can find a woman about the size of Minnie Mouse to wear it," she replied edgily. "Of course it's ruined." Alexis shook her head in disgust. "It was silk."

Angry now, he let his voice rise in response to hers. "Can't you accept a simple apology? What is it with you, anyway? Send me a bill."

"Come to think of it, I just might."

His brown eyes, ever alert, took on a humorous glint. "Then I'll send you mine for the hospital bill. We can wipe the slate clean."

"Your slate's so full, it won't erase anymore."

"I'm going to try one more time." Harper dramatically rolled his eyes. "I apologize. I had no idea that sprinkler system was going to come on."

"To quote you, Harper, 'If I believed that . . .'" She gave him a mean look.

"What can I do to convince you?" Harper threw his hands up into the air in a gesture of futility. She was turning this whole thing into some point of honor.

Despite the feelings of desire that she managed to keep concealed, Alexis couldn't hold her anger in check. "The same thing I can do to convince you that I'm telling the truth," she spat. "Absolutely nothing."

He saw how her eyes flashed as she spoke. There was unmistakable rage there. Perhaps he'd made some mistake. Perhaps he'd been wary too long.

In a gesture of reconciliation he put out his hand to her.

"Don't." She jumped back. "Just don't touch me," Alexis snapped, and then instantly regretted her angry reaction. She wanted to apologize, but what could she say?

He gritted his teeth and started away. "I'll see you at dinner."

"Yes, I suppose you will."

"Good-bye."

Stiffly, Harper walked to his room. The humorous mood he'd felt earlier had vanished and was replaced by a dark cloud of gloom. All the time he dressed, Harper thought about Alexis, the things that had occurred between them, and the things that had not.

If he were to follow his natural instincts right now, he would seize the moment and go back to her, force her to see that they'd both made some mistakes, but he was certain she wouldn't listen. He'd pushed things too far. He'd been afraid to trust a woman since his painful divorce, and as a result, he'd made a mess of things. He was afraid it had ruined something very, very special.

After he showered and shaved, he went to the telephone and dialed information and then jotted down a number.

"Is this the city library?" He paused, then started to rapidly explain what he wanted. "I'm a visitor to your city and I was wondering if you could help me out. It's an emergency of sorts, really. I need all the books you can find on old architecture and restoration." He softened his tone. "If you could help me,

I'd be very grateful. In fact, I'd like to make a donation to your library."

Alexis dressed in a plaid taffeta calf-length skirt designed with springlike pastel colors. Her top was of turquoise silk, short-sleeved and scoop-necked. Because it was so important that her clothes not project her somber mood, she'd planned a casual, yet totally feminine style for Miss Sally's dinner.

Despite the emotional turmoil she felt, she wanted to show nothing but a pleasant, relaxed attitude when she met the others. It would take a great deal of effort to fake it, but she knew she had to. Harper must never suspect how vulnerable she was to him right now. He must never learn how much power he held over her.

The entire time she dressed, Alexis thought about Harper. She hated herself for it, knew she was wrong, but she wished she'd invited him inside her room. She didn't know what would have happened. Maybe they would have fought again, picked up the pace of their seemingly constant bickering, but there was also the chance that something else might have happened between them. She wished she'd taken the chance to find out. Maybe then she could have regained control over her emotions.

Miss Sally was standing inside the door of the smallest dining room, looking radiant and lively. She wore a becoming lavender silk dress, and Alexis took note of the evening suits both Harper and Mr. Carson wore. The octogenarian saw to it that the four of them were seated at a center table where a lavish arrangement of yellow tulips served as the center-piece.

Alexis let her eyes stray every now and then over to Harper, and each time she did, she caught him looking at her. There was no warmth in his expression. Instead, he had a strange, brooding look, nothing at all like the smile he usually wore.

The evening proved to be strained and uncomfortable for everyone except Miss Sally. She seemed to be having her usual good time, filling in the conversational lags with stories about the hotel, about how the city had looked during the Confederacy, about her life as a young girl. Her stories were rich and exciting, but the group's mood was unreceptive.

It seemed to Alexis as if Mr. Carson were totally uninterested in Miss Sally's conversation and the people around him. He was the kind, she decided, who always did the right thing, was quite proper, but at the same time was always distant and cool.

As for Harper, he drank much more than she'd seen him do at any time before. His expression offered no clues to what he was thinking, but Alexis thought he must surely be furious.

And poor Miss Sally went on through the evening, determined to ignore the reactions of the others. She had an audience, albeit a less than enthusiastic one.

Alexis was trying to sort through her feelings about Harper. She'd tried to skirt the issue, ignore the potent attraction she felt toward the man; she'd even attempted to tell herself from time to time that nothing was happening between them. But she couldn't lie to herself, not for long.

When the evening was finally over, Miss Sally

walked them to the doors of the dining room. "I want all of you to join me on my sailboat tomorrow." She looked over at Mr. Carson. "I'll bet you're going to say you have to work. Aren't you?"

"I'm afraid I am," he nodded respectfully.

"Well, I won't take no from either one of you." She looked expectantly at Alexis and Harper.

Alexis cleared her throat and let her eyes stray to Harper. "I don't—"

"Oh, come now, you can't refuse an old lady," Miss Sally teased. "I'll have my driver pick you up at eleven-thirty. We'll meet at the boat and make a day of it. I have a wonderful sailor who'll make you glad you came along. Please don't say no," she cajoled.

"How can I refuse?" Alexis smiled.

"And you, Harper?"

It took all of his control to keep from looking at Alexis's face. The night had been as agonizing as he'd expected. The overpowering feelings of love that had taken over his life were not about to go away. The redheaded spitfire had his destiny right in the palm of her hand.

His lips tightened into a grimace, but then he said, "Of course."

"Good. Be out front at eleven-thirty."

The next morning passed quickly. Alexis stayed inside her room, preparing her bid on the hotel. Once, when she went downstairs into the lobby to re-count the number of dining room patrons who could be seated, she saw Harper, but they merely nodded to one another. Minutes before the designated time, Alexis completed her figuring, wrote out her proposal, and enclosed it in a long manila envelope. She put all her notes and the envelope inside her attaché case and locked it before she raced downstairs.

True to her word, Miss Sally had a car and a driver standing outside the hotel entrance, but Alexis found she was the only one there on time. She checked her bag, making sure she had her bathing suit and a change of clothes. She'd worn long white cotton pants and a matching sailor top, but the way the sun was shining made her ready to change into her suit right away.

She had a strange premonition when an employee of the hotel walked up to the driver and began to speak to him in hushed tones. She had the wildest urge to turn and run back inside the hotel.

"Miss Cartwright, I've just been told that Mr. Evans will meet us at the boat dock. Evidently, he's running a little late."

Alexis rode to the ramp in angry silence. She felt awkward and wondered what Harper possibly could be doing. It would have been much easier on her if she hadn't agreed to go on the excursion. Being around Harper was going to be difficult at best.

If that wasn't bad enough, when she arrived at the boat dock, she was met by the sailor friend of Miss Sally's, a sunburned man about her own age. As soon as he greeted her, he said he had a message for her and Mr. Evans but would wait until Harper arrived to deliver it. She wanted to scream. Everything was going haywire. The sailor walked away and she impatiently waited fifteen minutes, then twenty.

Irritated, she watched him return and told him,

"I'll wait a few minutes more and then if nobody else shows up, I'm leaving."

The sailor smiled at her, then looked over her shoulder. She followed the direction of his eyes.

"Hello." Harper rushed up wearing white shorts and a red polo shirt. As if he weren't almost half an hour late, he introduced himself to the sailor. "Where's Miss Sally?" he asked, carefully ignoring Alexis.

"Where have you been?" she asked. Her question was rude, but she was angry.

"Studying, if you must know." His icy look told her that she'd asked enough questions.

"Miss Sally is feeling a little under the weather today, and she asked me to tell you that she won't be able to join you. She said it might be from having too much fun last night." The sailor winked at Harper. "She said you'd understand about that."

"I do." Harper nodded. "Now what?"

"Well, sir, she's asked me to take the two of you for a sail. I've got a terrific picnic basket loaded down with food that she sent." He stopped. "There's only one little problem. I've promised a friend of mine I'd help him pull up the engine on his boat over there and it's been a bugger. He's in a real bind, and I feel like I need to help him, so it will be a little while, maybe an hour at most."

Harper glanced at Alexis and smiled. He had a mischievous look on his face. "I know how to sail. I've done it on and off for years."

"Interesting," she said with obvious disinterest.

"I'm not kidding." He laughed, making fun of her

136

coldness. He turned to the sailor. "Give us a minute, will you?"

"Sure." The sailor walked toward the boats docked next to them.

"What are you suggesting?"

Harper smiled. "That you and I take the boat out ourselves. I don't want to wait an hour. Do you?"

She eyed him. "Not particularly. In fact, I don't really want to go at all, but I'm afraid I might hurt dear Miss Ferguson's feelings." Alexis hesitated. "Why are you being so nice all of a sudden?"

"Nice?" He shaded his eyes with his hand against the full glare of the midday sun and turned away. "You wouldn't understand."

"Maybe not, but try me," she insisted.

"Maybe I've thought about yesterday and some other events, and just maybe I've decided that we ought to look at today as a whole new beginning." He felt an enormous urge to be alone with Alexis, and what better place than on a sailboat?

She frowned, and he began to laugh as if he'd only been teasing. "Like I said, you wouldn't understand. Anyway, I want to sail. Let's you and I give it a try. What do you have to lose?"

Alexis hesitated, then shrugged her shoulders. "Depending upon how good you really are at sailing, a lot!"

He laughed aloud again, and Alexis couldn't help but concentrate on the way his entire face lit up when he did. Damn it, there was that same attraction again, she thought. Would it ever go away?

"I told you I can sail," Harper bragged. "I'm really good at it." He began warming up to the subject.

"Anybody with half a brain can sail. All it takes is a few minutes of instruction—a few minutes, that's all."

"Uh huh." Alexis nodded. "One thing about it," she chided, "we could get this fiasco over with. Anybody who's as good a sailor as you say you are could get us out into the bay and back again before Miss Sally's man can even get ready to take us. Right?"

Harper took her arm and walked toward the sailor. "Your confidence is rewarding, to say the least, Miss Cartwright. I knew I'd have an interesting time today."

She grinned, surprised at the effect his touch was beginning to have on her. "Okay, show me what kind of skipper you are, but I warn you, I expect a calm, peaceful sailing experience. I've never done this before."

Alexis still felt a little resentment toward Harper for being so late as well as for a thousand other things, but she couldn't suppress a sense of pure excitement. She let herself fall in with his step.

Alexis was smart enough to know that she was playing with fire right now. She shouldn't go out on the boat with Harper, not when she was feeling so torn-up inside. She hadn't been able to sleep last night trying to sort through her feelings about him, but she was a stubborn woman and was confident she could take care of herself in any situation.

"Where is the boat?" Harper called to the sailor. "We've decided to take it out on our own. You don't mind, do you?"

The sailor grinned. "You sure you know how to handle her?"

"Not sure at all," Harper said under his breath, looking straight at Alexis. He nodded in the sailor's direction. "No problem."

"Want me to help you get off?"

"We can handle it." Harper looked around at the small sailboats docked around them. "Which one is it?"

"I'll take you to her. She's about the tenth boat down the line. Her name's *Miss Ebbtide.*"

"Fitting," Harper said, never letting go of Alexis's arm. "We'll find her. Go help your friend."

He'd said the right thing. The sailor didn't hesitate; he was ready to leave them. "Good luck. Holler back down if you need me."

Alexis and Harper started down the long pier. Harper put on his sunglasses. "We'll manage fine. Thanks."

"You sound like a first-class skipper," Alexis taunted. "I hope you are."

He tightened the grip on her arm and sped up. "Don't worry. I'm a lot better at sailing than you are at surfing."

"Very funny, Harper. You're just hilarious," she said dryly.

"Thanks. Sometimes I think so," he teased back.

He pulled her along as he counted the boats they passed. The breeze was perfect for sailing, he noticed.

"Wait up," Alexis protested. "Here it is."

Looking in the direction she was pointing, Harper took a deep breath and then let it out slowly. In big red letters he saw the name of the boat, *Miss Ebbtide.* Only it was no boat, it was a ship.

"Hell, this thing is . . ." he began, then thought

better of it. "I think there's been a mistake. I thought Miss Sally said it was a small boat."

"I never heard her say anything like that," Alexis answered, happy that the boat was so large. "Look, there's our picnic basket and an ice chest."

Harper realized he'd bragged a little too much. This sailboat looked as if a three-man crew was needed. "Uh, listen, I don't think . . ." His voice trailed off as he watched her climb aboard the boat and turn her face expectantly back to him.

"I'm going to tell the truth," Alexis said. "I was worried it would be one of those little dinky boats." She looked out across the wide expanse of blue water. "I feel a lot better now."

She was looking up at him, and he knew she was searching for a little reassurance. He drew in a deep breath again. This time he held it, as if the oxygen would clear his mind.

Finally, he spoke, jumping onto the boat. "Okay. We're off."

"What should I do?"

Harper wanted to smile at her willingness. She was a real sport, he thought, but if she only knew. He looked very serious as he tried to think what he wanted to do first.

Damnation! Nobody had told him how big this thing would be. He'd expected to find a tiny sailboat. Instead, he'd found a ship that could sail the Caribbean. If only there were a knowledgeable sailor aboard.

"Help me unfurl the sail," he said gruffly.

Luckily for him, the harbor was smooth and clear, and he was able to steer them out without much difficulty. Every time he thought he'd tell Alexis the truth about his sailing experience, the words wouldn't come out. They were getting along well, and he didn't want to risk her temper.

When they were away from the harbor, out on the gulf itself, where the water turned from pale turquoise to shimmering bright blue, Alexis said, "I'm glad I came. It's wonderful out here."

"You're not seasick or anything?" he asked.

"No, not a bit." She had gone down below and changed into her bathing suit, and now she stretched out across the deck, leaning her shoulders against the rail, letting her legs fall out in front of her.

Harper had taken off his shirt, and they sat in silence, letting the warming rays of the sun beam down on them and listening to the waves lap against the boat. He was relaxed again, glad to have been able to manage the boat as well as he had.

After a while Harper said, "I think I'll have a drink. Want one?"

"Here, I'll get it."

She slowly stood up and walked over to the ice chest. Her suit was a multicolored two-piece, and Harper studied the way she looked as she leaned over the ice chest and began telling him about the different choices they had. She reminded him of a fine racehorse, well bred and spirited, with a body and a brain to be admired.

He looked away when she held up a small bottle of wine in one hand and a beer in the other. He couldn't deny the emotions she aroused in him. He felt as if he would burst if he didn't tell Alexis how he felt about her.

"Wine. I'll take the wine," he said in a hoarse voice.

"I think we could stay out here for a week." Alexis opened the picnic basket. "There's enough food and drink for about eight people."

She walked toward him, opening up the chilled wine as she went. She had found a glass inside the picnic basket, and she began to pour the wine with care, her legs spread out to balance herself.

Suddenly aware that he hadn't been paying much attention to his sailing course, Harper looked ahead of them. A patch of rough water was directly in their path, and it was much too late to turn.

The wind began to blow the wine as Alexis poured it, sending drops of Chablis into the air to fall on Harper. She started to laugh, still balancing herself as she poured.

"Watch out," he called sternly, and she laughed harder, thinking it funny that he'd be bothered by a few drops of wine on his face.

The boat took a sharp rise and twisted to the right. Alexis began to fall forward, and Harper reached out to catch her. With the boat's next erratic move, she spilled the cold wine all over Harper's chest. He let go of the rudder, and the boat twisted sharply to the left.

"Get down," he shouted, grabbing Alexis and dragging her down with him.

The boat swayed back and forth, the rudder moving on its own in a zigzag pattern and the sail swinging itself about. Harper held Alexis to him, his body stretched out across hers, and despite the predicament they were in, he found himself responding to the softness of her skin and the way her legs brushed against his. She was crushed against him and he could feel the smooth flesh of her abdomen meeting his, and he knew that it would take everything he had just to move away from her.

He pulled himself to alertness and reached up to grab the rudder, bringing it under control after a few seconds. "Sorry," he breathed, watching the way she lay there, her face full of surprise.

"What happened?" she asked breathlessly. She watched the way he took command of the rudder again, bringing the power of his shoulders and arm muscles into play. Her heart was hammering, and she felt a hard constriction there. She wasn't sure whether she was more concerned about the boat or the way she was feeling about Harper right now.

"It's okay. We just hit a patch of rough water."

Slowly, it dawned on her as she watched him study the sail and maintain the rudder. He wasn't at all the experienced sailor he'd claimed to be.

"Anybody with half a brain can sail, huh?" she said grimly, and stood up. "Tell me, are you using the right or the left half? Whichever side it is, it's obviously the wrong one."

"Alexis, get me a glass of wine and I'll explain," he said softly, keeping his eyes on the water ahead.

"Are you sure it's safe?"

He nodded.

After she'd gotten both of them a drink, she waited. He didn't look at her but kept his eyes steadily ahead.

"I know how to sail. I've done it a lot of times," he

began, as the wind picked up. "And, besides, we can use the engine if the wind dies down."

She sat close to him so that she could hear, trying not to think about how long and muscular his legs looked or the way the sun caught the dark hairs on his legs and chest and made them shine. She was only now beginning to breathe with any regularity.

"Rubber boats in the bathtub, I bet."

"No, real boats. Only they weren't quite as big as this one."

Something in the way he'd confessed, like a little boy who'd been caught in a white lie, made her laugh.

He grinned. "I should have told you before, but . . ." He watched her as she kept laughing, and finally he began to laugh, too.

"It's too late now, isn't it?" She chuckled, pointing to the distant shoreline. She became serious for a second. "Can you get us back there?" Her eyes grew wide.

He nodded. "I'm still a better sailor than you are a surfer."

"Oh, is that so?" she challenged.

"Yeah, at least I haven't hit myself on the head yet." He grinned.

"I'd like to do that part for you, but I don't want to be out here by myself. Even having you around is better than nothing."

"Okay." He held up his hand. "I declare a truce, effective here and now." Dramatically, he put out his hand. "Let's share a pleasant hour together, Alexis."

She looked at him for a long time, aware of how desperately she wanted him to kiss her the way he

144

had once before. Had too much passed between them? She really didn't know. She nodded.

"Here are the ground rules. We do not discuss the hotel. We can tell anything we want about ourselves, discuss anything except business." His voice softened. "We can do anything we want to do. There's just you and me."

"I just want to say one thing before we begin." She took a deep swallow of the Chablis.

"Go ahead."

"You are the most pigheaded, obnoxious man I have ever met."

He stared at her, a smile playing around the corners of his lips. "And you, my dear lady, have a head as hard as knotty pine."

She went over to the picnic basket. "Now that we've got that over with, do you want something to eat?"

"Has our truce begun yet?" He drained his drink. "Because if it has, I want to tell you that I've been thinking about us." He watched her, seeing how she avoided looking at him. He changed his mind. Now wasn't the time. "Someday I'll tell you what I think. Someday when you're ready to listen."

"Let's eat," she insisted, caught off-guard by his words and the emotions they stirred up within her.

"And then what?" he returned smoothly.

CHAPTER EIGHT

The man absolutely drained Alexis of any self-assurance she had ever possessed. She found herself shaking inside from his words as well as his presence. More than anything she wanted to find out what it was he had wanted to say to her, but she stubbornly resolved to keep her distance. She was a fool to be out here with him, she thought. There was no need to make things worse than they already were.

"Let's see," she said, trying her best to sound casual. "I think there's some smoked turkey and cheese inside the hamper." She began giving the contents of the basket an unusually long study. "It looks like we have sliced turkey, ham, cheese, dill pickles, and two kinds of bread."

"And it looks like it's time to tighten up the sail and rest for a while. We've gone out just about as far as I think we should." Harper went about his duties with the sure, confident air she'd come to admire.

The shoreline was like a faraway speck, making Alexis feel even more alone than she had at first. She felt the sun beam down on her and the breeze caress her skin like a lover's gentle kiss.

Harper began to talk to her as they ate. Sounding much like he had when they first met, he casually told her bits and pieces about himself. After her sandwich, and another glass of wine were gone, Alexis found herself relaxed and content. Hearing his voice and being with him in such calm, peaceful surroundings lulled her into reliving the memories of their first kiss.

"A penny for your thoughts."

She shrugged lazily. "They're worth much more than that."

"I'm sure they are," Harper said, reaching into the picnic basket.

He was sitting close, his leg so near hers that she could feel the warmth of his body. A dark cloud passed overhead, and she noticed a sudden burst of cool wind.

"You know, when I was a kid, I used to stretch out on the ground, out behind our barn and watch the clouds roll by. I'd try to imagine what each cloud looked like. I created the most wonderful things, especially right before a storm." Harper lifted his eyes skyward. "I had all kinds of Indians and cowboys and spacemen parading before me, and then, quick as a wink, they'd disappear."

"You know, the night you and I went to dinner together, I knew you had a rich imagination. It's your use of language, I think." She looked up at the sky, too. The clouds were rolling much faster than they'd done earlier.

"I knew something about you then, too, Alexis. I just didn't want to admit it to myself."

Totally relaxed, she sighed. "I'd be lying if I said I wasn't curious to know what it was."

He remained silent for so long, she thought he

wasn't going to respond. His eyes were closed, his arms were crossed behind his head, and his mouth was tightly compressed.

The wind blew stronger, cooling the air around the sailboat. The water's waves grew larger. He sniffed the air. It smelled of rain.

"I knew you were special," he let himself say. "I knew you were very, very special." The words seemed to hover around them for seconds, as if waiting for an answer.

Harper opened his eyes and looked at her. She met his look head-on, knowing that the emotions they both felt must be dealt with at some point.

Her breath quickened, then caught in her throat as he brought one hand down to rest on her arm. When he looked at her again, she recognized his message, of desire, of need.

"Alexis, I . . ." Harper stopped. It had turned dark all around them. Big raindrops began to fall, and the wind whistled by, whipping against their bodies. "Help me get the sail anchored safely," he said with a trace of tension in his voice.

"Tell me what to do." The wind was cold against her skin, and she knew there was no time for thinking, only reacting.

"It's only a storm cloud, not even a squall," she heard him call as they struggled with the endless expanse of sail. "It'll be gone as fast as it came. Five minutes at the most."

"My, you're full of good news," she managed, almost falling into the sail.

"Be careful. It's very important that you maintain your footing, Alexis."

"Yeah, I think you're right." She was holding on to the sail with all her might, knuckles whitened with the strain. She watch Harper with his back to her as he headed for the rudder.

The boat continued its tossing, responding to the abrupt surge of wind, and the water, which had taken on a malevolence all its own, rising and foaming, capping and swirling. Alexis got her balance and then began to follow Harper.

Suddenly, something slammed into her midsection and she went down. The next thing she knew, she was in the churning water, trying to see where she was. It had been the boom that hit her, she realized as she frantically tried to stay afloat.

Harper yelled, "Hold out your arm. I'll help you."

She didn't panic, although she wanted to. Instead, she did as he'd commanded. But when he reached out and almost had her fingertips, she saw the boat tip sideways and then Harper himself was overboard.

She told herself when it was all over, she would laugh whenever she remembered the look of awe on his face. Right now she used calm, steady strokes to swim toward him, grateful for his strength and sound thinking. He still had a grip on the boat.

"Hold on to me," he called, and she swam against the powerful water until she felt his cold fingers. The ocean's spurt of insanity was weakening; even the rain had stopped.

"I'm going to lift you up and you swing over into the boat. Then you can help me. We're going to have to cooperate. Don't let go of me, Alexis."

She nodded, wondering if he noticed she had a death grip on his wrist. "Okay, I'm ready."

He took one of her hands and put it on the edge of the boat, carefully making sure she had a good grip. Then using his free hand he reached down and cupped her buttocks, and she felt the power of his arm as he hoisted her up and over.

She fell into the boat, landing with most of her weight on one shoulder blade and an elbow. There was no time to worry about the pain she was feeling.

"Now me," Harper yelled, and then he smiled assuringly as if this were a perfectly ordinary thing for them to be doing.

She reached out for his arm and, with her other hand, grabbed him just below his ribcage and pulled. She saw that his chest was scraping against the side of the boat, but he never said a word.

When he fell into the boat, they both lay there for a long while, taking time to get their breath. The storm cloud passed by and the sun returned, although soon it would begin to go down in the western horizon. Except for the memory of their experience, there was no sign that anything had happened.

"You're dangerous."

"Me!" she exclaimed, and then began to laugh. "That's a little like the pot calling the kettle black. I never claimed I could sail a boat."

"Maybe not, but have you noticed that whenever you're around I end up in trouble?" He was teasing. His lips curved up into a grin, and his eyes twinkled. He'd almost gotten them into a disastrous situation, but now that it was all over, his good humor was returning.

"That's so preposterous I won't even try to answer

you." She watched him sit up, pulling her with him. "Now we're even. If we live through this, that is."

"We're even?" He held up the picnic basket, and they watched the water drip steadily from the bottom of the wicker. "How do you figure?"

"I'll accept a little blame for trying to show off on my surfboard the other day if you'll accept responsibility for showing off today."

They looked at one another. She was shivering with cold. Her hair hung down around the edge of her face in tiny half-curls. His teeth were beginning to chatter, and big red gashes ran across his chest where he'd scraped against the boat. Spontaneously, they burst into wild laughter.

"A deal, although my pride tells me I should plead the fifth amendment," he answered when their laughter had died down.

"Just tell me one little thing, Harper. Would you, please?"

He reached into the ice chest and pulled out two bottles of wine. "If I can."

"Are we going to be able to make it to shore?"

"Yes. Look how close we are. When we're ready, we can sail straight in. Okay?"

She looked at the shoreline, noting how much nearer it seemed. "Okay. That's all I wanted to know."

He opened the bottles and handed one to her. "I'm afraid the glasses are broken."

"One more question, Harper." She cupped both hands around the bottle.

"Only one?"

"For now."

"I'm fortifying myself. Your questions aren't like other people's questions." Lifting the bottle to his lips, he drank half of it.

"Ready?"

"Now I'm ready," he said, grinning. "Go ahead."

"Are we ever going to warm up?"

"That's your question?" It wasn't what he'd expected. He looked down at her, aware of the slight blue tinge rimming her lips. "Do you want to head for shore? I can turn us around right now."

She let the words sink in, never taking her eyes off him. Something in his voice warned her that the question was an important one. Once more their eyes met, and she did not turn away.

"Look, you're about to be rescued. I believe it's Miss Sally's sailor friend." Harper watched a motorboat approach.

The sailor called out to them, and Harper answered. Then he turned back to Alexis.

"Now or never. It's your chance. We can go in now."

If she said yes they could return to the hotel and perhaps end up as casual acquaintances who'd shared a few interesting moments. She licked her lips pensively, feeling his eyes bore through her, as if he were challenging her to stay with him. Was he offering her their last chance to explore whatever it was that existed between them? she wondered.

Alexis knew what her answer had to be. She could no longer deny that she felt very deeply about Harper. She wanted to be with him and wouldn't let herself think past that point. She considered herself a realist, but even a realist should be allowed a blind spot or two. She knew where hers was. He was standing only inches away.

Gathering up her courage, she asked, "What do you have in mind?"

"You tell me," he returned smoothly. He didn't move.

She hesitated a moment, but still the sensations flaming inside her demanded their own satisfaction.

"Lady's choice. Shall I head for home?" He was determined not to make it easy for her. He'd been the one who'd searched her out, tried to maintain some semblance of communication between them over the past few days. Now it was her choice whether to go on or not.

"Right now I'm just wondering if I can get warmed up if I stay." Her voice rose and fell with the implication of her words, and she wondered at herself.

"I believe so."

"All right. I'll stay," she said slowly.

He wanted to take her into his arms yet felt he mustn't. He wouldn't push Alexis in any way, Harper decided. He would let things progress at their own rate.

"I—I'm going below and see if there's a towel. Then I'm coming back and drying you off." He waved away the sailor, telling him they'd watch the sunset and then come in.

Harper went below, and Alexis watched the small boat move away from them. She started to follow Harper down and then changed her mind. Slow and easy, she thought, and she waited.

The sun had lost its power and was sliding down to

meet the horizon. Across the sky were bright ribbons of orange and blue.

"We may have a soggy picnic basket, but look what I have," Harper's voice boomed out from below. He returned with two towels, a box of saltine crackers, more wine, and a slab of slightly green cheese.

After wrapping themselves in the towels, they devoured the food as if they hadn't eaten in days. Once the chill was gone, Alexis felt comfortable, except for her shoulder and elbow. They were becoming more painful by the minute.

Sitting upon the foredeck of the cabin, Harper asked Alexis about growing up in the family of the famous A. B. Cartwright. After she'd told him all the humorous stories she could think of, her thoughts became more serious.

Harper was stretched out on his side, propping up his head on one arm, holding his wine bottle with his other hand. He'd turned the boat toward the shoreline, and they were slowly drifting back toward land. Alexis lay stretched out across the wooden planking, one leg bent, her head elevated by the two towels they'd used to dry themselves.

"You know, my father was devoted to his family. He idolized my mother. He'd do anything for her, and he treated Abra and me like we were the most special of the special."

"I can tell."

She eyed him quizzically. "How?"

"There's something about you, Alexis, that makes me know you've been loved. There's something beneath all those beautiful clothes and that finishing school poise. I can't describe it. It just exists."

His words flooded her with a warmth she longed to hold on to. She closed her eyes.

"But there's something else, too."

She turned toward him.

"Evidently, you have a need to prove yourself. Why's that?"

She'd been right the first time she'd met him. This man was much more complex than he seemed to be.

"Do you have any idea what it's like to be thought of as an appendage—like someone's arm or finger? Do you know how it feels to be raised by someone who's loving and caring but at the same time is so dominating that you sometimes feel as if he's smothering you? My sister, Abra, says we were both born too smart. Sometimes I wonder!"

He nodded his understanding. "Living with a legend?"

"Exactly. We were never looked at by anyone as anything except A. B. Cartwright's daughters. That's as far as our identities went." She took a breath. "It wasn't his fault. God knows he did the best he could. So did my mother, but people wouldn't let us be anything else."

Harper reached behind him and brought out another small bottle of wine. "And so you've struck out on your own, and that's why you resented my thinking you were using your father's money."

She nodded. "It's important to me. That's all." A thought struck her. "Yet, when I talk to you about it, I know that what those other people think is not really all that important after all. I know I've done it on my own. That should be enough."

Harper put down his wine bottle and held her hand

in his, caressing her gently. She let her fingers respond, running lightly around the ridge of his thumb and downward into the curve of his hand. She was buoyed by the aura of affection and caring that so obviously existed between them.

"I hope this won't make you angry, Alexis, but you and I are very much alike." He waited for her to respond.

"How so?" she asked, not angry in the least, merely curious.

"We've both spent an awful lot of wasted time worrying about other people's feelings. I know I should have been taking responsibility for my behavior."

"I don't understand what you mean, Harper." She was more and more aware of the tempting warmth of his hand.

"I mean that my ex-wife caused me a lot of trouble, and ever since our divorce I've distrusted every woman I've met. That was wrong. I know it now. Everything that's happened between you and me was all shadowed by my distrust, not of you but of my ex-wife."

Alexis looked down at his hand, which completely covered hers. She was afraid that if she looked at Harper she might cry. His words affected her so deeply, she wasn't even sure how she might react.

When she was able, she answered him. "Maybe you're right." Her voice had a slight quaver.

Somehow she was able to look at things differently today, perhaps more clearly. Everything suddenly seemed much more simple than before. Harper seemed magically able to put things in perspective for her.

"Ohh," she moaned when she tried to stretch upward.

"What's the matter?"

She lay back down, twisting herself onto her side. "It's my shoulder blade. I think I really hurt it."

"Let me see," Harper insisted, sitting up on his knees. With careful, steady fingers he began to probe the tender flesh around her shoulder.

"It hurts right there." The air whistled through her clenched teeth.

"It's turning black and blue all right. I saw some liniment down in the galley. I'll be right back."

He ignored her feeble protest, and when he returned, he brought with him a body-length cushion from somewhere below. "Here we go." He helped her turn over on her stomach.

She felt his fingers untie the thin bikini straps, but the strong smell of the liniment caught her attention. She looked at him questioningly. "Is that for humans? It smells like it came out of a horse stable."

"The smell will go away fast. Don't worry." He began to rub away her aches, and his touch felt so good that she closed her eyes and grew quiet.

His moves were unpredictable, unpatterned, yet warm and soothing, and Alexis felt herself relax more with his every stroke. Gentle and enticing, his hands continued to knead her tender flesh.

She tried to swing her thoughts in a million different directions. Nothing worked. All she could concentrate on was the way she felt when she was near him, and the air of anticipation which clung to them, becoming stronger and stronger until she felt she might choke on it. Alexis realized that his gentle massage was only a prelude. She shuddered.

"Something wrong?" He bent down and touched his lips to her bruised back.

She stiffened against the ache that spread from her shoulder throughout her body and forced herself to forget their life back on shore, relegating all the problems in their relationship to some distant corner of her mind.

He continued to kiss her back gently, teasingly, making her weak with desire. This was what she'd known would happen, what she wanted to happen. When she felt him running his fingers lightly across the tender surface of the back of her legs, she knew she could no longer hope to resist.

Alexis turned over in slow motion, fiercely aware of the sensual pull that drew her to him. She brushed away the last remaining doubt as she reached up to encircle his neck in unrestrained desire.

As he brought his arms around her, pulling her to him, Alexis felt her desire grow even stronger. She met his lips with a passion that surprised even herself, and reveled in the warmth of his probing, intimate kiss.

He took his time, although she could all too clearly sense the urgency of his desire. Seductively, he molded his mouth to hers as she ran her fingers along the tendons of his neck and felt the fiery warmth of his skin.

There was a hunger in her—one she'd tried to deny from the beginning. Now she acknowledged it, along with the fierce passion she'd held back. She felt a churning inside her, building up and up with each caress, each movement he made. All the suppressed tensions and passion came to a boil as her tongue met his. Inside his mouth, she could taste the remnants of the wine, and her tongue raced to explore the depths of the unknown.

He pulled away and looked at her for a second, then brought his hands down in a straight line from the softest points of her neck to the peaks of her breasts. He kissed the imaginary line he'd traced.

She sucked in her breath then, not from fear or withdrawal but from a white-hot sensation deep within her.

He bent down and kissed her again, parting her lips with his tongue, beginning another exploration. Then he moved and stretched his long body out beside hers on the cushion.

She could feel the heat, the mounting intensity between them as his body came nearer and nearer. It was as though they were on fire, consumed by the same flame.

Eyes tightly shut, she felt him lift his lips away from hers, and then he was bringing her hand up to stroke his sensuous lips. She felt his warm kiss, first in the soft center of her palm and then fanning out toward the pulse point of her wrist.

The fierce flush of her need felt like a potent tropical storm building to a crescendo. She brought one leg toward his, running her foot up and down the calf of his leg in tantalizingly slow motions.

From far, far away, Alexis heard his voice, low and rawly disturbing. "I love you, Alexis."

She felt his body move, and she turned ever so slightly to meet his movements, bringing her leg in between his. She heard him moan then, and with one brief movement, he pushed the top of her bathing suit aside.

Alexis felt more alive than she ever had before. Her responses were immediate and instinctive, beginning not in thought but in pure need. It was as if she were inside a magnificent kaleidoscope, moving, whirling, spinning all around.

Harper's lips continued to torment her, moving from the sensitive skin of her wrist to her throat, coaxing her, urging a greater and greater response from her. The pleasure was exquisite, and she let her hips weave slowly against his, feeling the fiery need in him, responding with tender kisses of her own along his hairline, his neck, and down his upper back.

He held her captive, beginning once again to trail light kisses all along her inner arm. It was as if a million nerves were gathered there in the soft inner core of her flesh, waiting to be awakened by the touch of his tongue.

She kissed the fleshy lobe of his ear and reached up in desperation to pull him to her.

"Oh, Harper, please," she begged, seeking mercy and relief from the delicate torture he was inflicting upon her. She was going out of her mind with desire.

He could feel her tremble and it pleased him. They were evenly matched now. There was no competition, no differences—only a woman and a man. His lips caressed the softest part of her upper arm, lingering, savoring the luxurious feel of her, then he drew circles with his mouth across and over to the swell of her bare breast.

She couldn't be still. Her body was controlling its

own course, demanding satisfaction. Her legs wrapped around him, and her hips twisted and strained toward his.

He kissed the peak of her breast, and with heated anticipation she waited for him to do more. Soon she felt his moist, warm tongue flicker against the lower part of her breast. The sensation made her long to scream out.

She reached up for him, trying to press her entire body against his; she wanted to meld herself to him, to become one with him.

He lifted himself away. With firm but gentle movements he withdrew the bottom of her suit, catching it up in his fingers and slowly easing it down over her feet. The feel of the night's cool air striking her heated body sent a wave of chill through her, and she desperately gripped his arms.

Tenderly he lay her back down, sending warm kisses along the lines where the suit had been. She bit her lips, stifling a weak moan.

How much more could she bear? Alexis wondered as she watched him strip away his shorts. She brought her head up and placed it against his chest, burrowing her face in the coarse dark hair, kissing away the pain from the long red scratches where he'd skinned himself on the boat.

Harper held her there and lifted his face to the heavens. At last he had what he'd dreamed of for so long. He bent down and kissed the top of her head.

With each movement it was as if they were unraveling the mysteries of life together. She was relying upon the strength of her instincts, discovering a powerful eroticism within her that she had never known existed. With each new wave of sensation she made profound discoveries, both about herself and about Harper. Somewhere in the back of her mind she knew she would never be the same woman she'd been before, and she was glad.

When he finally lowered his body down upon hers, she moaned in pleasure and pushed her hips up to meet him. Urgency seized her, and she wrapped her hands around his head, stroking his hair over and over again.

She wanted to take the time to respond to all the sensations his body aroused within hers, but they had gone too far. In the distant corners of her mind she was aware of the way his ribcage pressed against hers, of the coarse hair of his chest rubbing against her sensitive breasts, and of the heat of his body as they moved together.

She was vaguely aware of the rocking lull of the water, the darkness which now hung over them, and the twinkling lights from the distant shore. But these held no meaning for her now. Time and place meant nothing. Reason and thought had been forgotten.

She felt herself on the edge, the sheerest edge, pausing momentarily, then falling with a heady rush into that one blinding, compelling wave of abandon, and then a warm, midnight haze consumed her.

And afterward, when the glow still refused to abate, Alexis curled into his arms, warm, still absorbed in the sensations that raged through her body. She listened to him whisper loving words, and she stared up into the moonlight. There was no tomorrow. Only now.

CHAPTER NINE

Shortly before midnight, they maneuvered the sailboat back to the dock. Harper worked hard, trying to keep it from banging into anything, his sailing skills still not very trustworthy. Watching him scamper from one side of the boat to the other, a worried expression on his face, Alexis couldn't keep herself from laughing.

"If you'd spend a little more time helping and a little less making fun of a poor, exhausted sailor, we'd both be better off," he muttered.

Heeding his words, she tried to help, but every time she looked at him, she began to laugh. Since they had made love, their mood had changed. They had become completely relaxed, carefree, and playful with each other.

He came around beside her and gave her a light tap on the shoulder, gesturing for help with the folding of the sail. "I knew I should have left you out in the water the other day. You might have been rescued by some handsome young beach bum."

"And miss all this fun? Not on your life," she teased.

"Let's tie it up, and we're through."

They walked along the dock toward the street,

contentedly holding hands. In and out of the darkness they continued to the corner, their voices ringing out in the night.

"Mr. Evans," a voice called out from a car parked near the curb.

Harper tightened his grip on her fingers and moved protectively in front of her. "Yes."

"Miss Sally sent me down after you and Miss Cartwright. She said I was to wait for you." The driver got out of the car and opened the back door for them, smoothing his hair back as if he'd been caught napping.

"That was thoughtful of her." Alexis got into the back, and Harper eased in beside her, his arm wrapped around her.

The driver started off, and Harper leaned down and gently kissed Alexis. For the first time in many hours, Alexis's thoughts returned to the present and the problems she faced.

"Did you know that when Houston was still swampland, Galveston was full of quarter-million-dollar homes and the finest goods straight from New York?"

Harper felt a twinge of tension in her, and he squeezed her arm. "No, I didn't. Who told you that? Miss Sally?"

She went on, ignoring his feeble joke. "In 1900, Galveston was the second richest city in the entire country."

"Well, it's gone downhill since then," he said, looking at the dismal structures lined along the beachfront.

When they approached the lighted hotel, Alexis

stared up at the turrets and spires, absorbed by the way their intricate designs made strange, elongated shadows in the darkness. It was too much, the thought of tearing all this down.

The elevator ride was quiet. Harper realized that the magic that had occurred between them on the boat was gone. Whether it could be recaptured or not was yet to be seen. He reached over and pulled her to him, his lips grazing her shoulder. The elevator creaked noisily, and he was reminded of how they had met. He kissed her again.

"I can't keep my hands off you." He sighed and, perceiving no response, reluctantly leaned his head back against the elevator wall.

As much as she wanted to respond to his words, Alexis couldn't. Returning to the hotel had brought her back to reality. She was only too aware that no matter what had happened between them personally, they were still combatants, both wanting the same thing but for totally different reasons. Everything she looked at was a reminder, everything she touched.

When they stepped out on the sixth floor, she ran her fingers along the brass switch plates next to the elevator. Suddenly, she was tired, completely exhausted.

"Do you have your key?" Harper extended his hand as they approached her door. He unlocked it and smiled softly at her, knowing Alexis was drifting far away from him.

He stepped back. "Did you know that Galveston was once known as the Grand Dame of the Gulf?"

She watched him, trying to decide if his words carried any more meaning than mere end-of-the-evening conversation. She twisted the doorknob and stepped inside.

Moodily, she said, "There's a chance to bring a little of that beauty back to the island, Harper."

He brought her hand up to his lips, and she felt a warm rush of desire spin through her as he kissed the inside of her palm. It was almost like reliving their moments together on the boat, she thought as her heart beat more quickly at the memory.

"You're the most beautiful thing that this island has seen since it was created by the sea." He turned and walked slowly away until he reached the corner of the hallway. "I'm going to woo you, Alexis. Wait and see. Like a true Galveston gentleman should." He smiled, his brown eyes alert and clear. "Wait and see."

She shut the door behind her and headed for the shower. Tonight wasn't the time to worry about what they'd done. The memory would be tarnished soon enough, when they met tomorrow to decide once and for all who would own the Ebbtide and what the hotel's future would be.

After her shower she wanted nothing more than sleep, but she had to set her alarm. The morning would be upon her too soon. Turning on the bedroom light, she noticed a familiar scent in the air, reminding her of Harper and his delicious manly scent.

She promised herself she'd go to sleep remembering everything about the man on the sailboat, the man she knew she loved. Yet the fact that their futures would be irreversibly changed in a matter of hours preyed heavy on her mind. Even her memories of the electrifying moments she'd spent with Harper couldn't erase her worry completely.

"Hey . . ." Alexis saw her attaché case on the table where she'd left it, but there was a deep scratch on the side of the case, one she wouldn't have noticed if the light hadn't caught it just right.

She unlocked the case and peered in, trying to remember exactly how she'd left the contents. Carefully, Alexis picked up the envelope that contained her bid and held it up to the lamplight before turning it slowly over in her fingers. Moving nearer the light, she studied the seal on the envelope. It was dried and loose in places, not at all tightly shut the way she'd left it.

She felt the edges of the seal. The envelope had been opened and resealed, she was certain. She opened the bid and glanced through it, but nothing had been changed. Somebody had wanted to know what her bid was to be.

Quickly, she went to the closet and opened the door then she checked the lock on her hotel room door. Someone had been inside her room, had opened her attaché case and read the bid she intended to make on the Ebbtide. Someone wanted to beat her and was willing to commit a crime in order to do so.

An icy chill ran through her as she stood in the middle of the room, clutching the open envelope in her hand. There were only two possibilities. Harper or Mr. Carson. Who else could have done it?

If it had been Harper, had he hired an accomplice, or was that the reason he'd been so late meeting her at the boat dock this morning? Alexis sat down on the bed, her mind reeling. Picking up the pillow, she hugged it close to her, seeking some sort of comfort. She sank her face into the soft cushion, trying to calm herself.

From the start Harper had been a tough, aggressive businessman. He'd never bothered to conceal his reasons for wanting the Ebbtide. He'd used his natural charisma, his good looks, and his warm brand of humor to charm first Alexis and then Miss Sally. When he'd discovered there was a possibility that Alexis might buy the hotel, he'd become furious, making angry threats, wildly promising her that he would end up the Ebbtide's owner. Clearly, he'd wanted no opposition whatsoever, particularly from her.

Coldly, she recalled all the events of the week. This morning he'd been late for the sailing adventure, telling her when she'd pressed for an explanation that he'd been studying. Studying my bid, she fumed. What else could he have meant?

The final question dealing with Harper was the most difficult, but one she had no choice but to ask herself. Had his seduction of her been part of the plan?

She twisted around and stretched back across the bed, caught up in the dark velvet memories of his touch. It couldn't be. Surely no one was that accomplished an actor. Too much had passed between them. She had felt it.

It hurt so much to think that Harper might have betrayed her that she closed the possibility from her mind and concentrated on Mr. Carson. He seemed a likely suspect if only because he'd been so enigmatic from the very beginning.

Alexis believed in her instincts, and from the first time she'd met him, there'd been something about Mr. Carson that had disturbed her. It wasn't anything he said. He said very little. No, it had been something else. His quiet, almost condescending attitude, his strange comings and goings, and then his cold lack of interest in involving himself with any of them, all added up to make him immensely suspicious.

She couldn't remember how many times she'd wanted to talk to Harper about Mr. Carson. Every time she'd been around the mysteriously aloof man, she'd wanted to approach Harper with her doubts, but it seemed they were always at odds with one another, tightly embroiled in their own battle, and she'd ended up with no one to talk to.

Finally, she reached up and turned out the light, then kicked back the covers and crawled into bed. She could hear the clock ticking away persistently, bringing her closer and closer to the time when she'd find out who'd been in her room. She pulled the sheet up around her and tucked it under her chin.

Alexis felt heartbroken and defeated when she realized she'd probably lost the Ebbtide forever. The tears finally came, stinging her eyes, falling across the bridge of her nose and down onto the pillow. When she was very still, it seemed as though she could hear them.

Whoever read her bid knew how much she had planned to pay for the hotel. No matter what else happened, she'd lost her edge. Whoever beat her bid tomorrow would be the guilty party.

During the night, as she drifted in and out of a

deeply troubled sleep, Alexis told herself again and again, almost like a silent prayer, that Harper hadn't been the guilty one. He was the man she loved.

When her alarm went off the next morning, she burrowed her head back into the sanctuary of her pillow and dozed. She hadn't had nearly enough sleep, and when she finally forced herself to get up, there was no time for a shower. She intended to be the first one in Miss Sally's apartment. She hoped there'd be some sort of telltale sign when Harper and Mr. Carson entered the room.

It didn't take her long to dress. She chose a tailored, black-and-white knit Castleberry suit, off-black hose, and patent-leather heels. Black onyx earrings circled in pavé diamonds finished off the look she wanted for the day, that of a capable, coolheaded businesswoman.

Miss Sally greeted her, giving her a gentle hug and leading her into the living area. "I'm so glad you're here first, Alexis, dear, because I've been dying to know if you and Harper had a good time yesterday out on the boat?"

Alexis took the comfortable seat Miss Sally offered her, glancing around the elegantly furnished room.

"Yes," she replied, "we did have a good time."

"I'm so glad." The older woman's eyes twinkled and she gave Alexis a tender smile. "I like the idea of you two being together."

Alexis reached down and adjusted the handle on her briefcase. She didn't want to be reminded of yesterday, not right now.

"Oh, I see you brought your attaché case. I re-

170

member how our Mr. Carson found it so interesting that you didn't carry one with you everywhere," Miss Sally observed. "I'll get us some coffee."

That was it! When Miss Sally began to talk about Mr. Carson, Alexis remembered it all, too. Mr. Carson was the one who, right here in this room, had started up that strange conversation with Alexis about her attaché case.

Absentmindedly, Alexis fingered one gold earring. In fact, when Mr. Carson had brought up the discussion about her use of an attaché case, Alexis had thought it particularly funny because it was the longest conversation he'd bothered to conduct with her.

She leaned her head back against the chair. Oh, please, she screamed out in her head, let it be Mr. Carson. Facing a betrayal by Harper was too much for her troubled mind to handle. It just couldn't be.

A bird flew by the window, floating on the air currents with ease, a powerful reminder of what Alexis already knew. She was going to lose this place without ever having it.

She grieved for the loss, and yet she knew her reasons were very different now than they had been the first day she came. She realized she didn't need to own the hotel to show anyone what she could accomplish. Whatever else he might have done, Harper had helped her see that. But nevertheless, she grieved for the beauty that could be resurrected. The Ebbtide deserved far better than destruction.

Taking the coffee Miss Sally handed her, Alexis looked up into the old woman's face. "You're going to miss this place, aren't you?" she asked.

"With all my heart." The woman's voice cracked when she spoke.

"I will, too," Alexis whispered.

The emotion of the moment was lost when there was a knock at the door. Alexis felt a moment of sheer panic, then she regained her composure, straightened her skirt, and casually crossed her legs. What would be, would be.

"Good morning, Mr. Carson. My, but you're very prompt," Miss Sally welcomed him.

Wasn't it funny that no one even knew his first name? Alexis thought, watching him enter the living room. In the morning light Mr. Carson looked like a very different man than she'd seen before, and Alexis studied his eyes and his manner, trying to decide what he was really like.

There was a certain new look about him, Alexis could tell. She could have sworn that Mr. Carson's eyes almost gleamed with satisfaction as he walked through the room. Dressed in an expensive blue pin-stripe suit, his step was brisk and animated. He shook her hand, avoiding eye contact.

A tingle ran all through her body. Was she noticing these things because they were real, or because she wanted so desperately to make them real? The tension built inside her. She couldn't make a final judgment just yet.

Mr. Carson was already seated across from her, busily studying something inside his attaché case when Harper entered. Alexis held her head down, feeling a flush race to her face. She didn't think she could bear to look at him.

"Good morning everyone. I'm sorry if I'm late for

172

the big event. It seems I'm late everywhere I go lately." His rumbly voice brought the room to life.

Carson spoke, and Miss Sally poured him coffee. Distractedly, Alexis rubbed the back of her hand across her eyes. She didn't want to look up.

"Miss Sally, I'm sorry you couldn't make it yesterday, but I want you to know I had the most wonderful day of my life. That boat of yours is really something. Don't you agree, Alexis?"

Everyone waited, and she knew she had to say something. She brought her head up, her eyes seeking his, and when she did, a new wave of sensations flooded over her. Harper was smiling, but when she looked up at him, Alexis saw his smile grow broader, and then he laughed a bit uncertainly.

"Well, maybe I'm the only one who thought the day was that important." He watched Alexis's face. "I'll admit I'm not the sailor I thought I was. That was quite a boat."

He was dressed in a finely cut light gray suit and a white silk shirt. His eyes shone with excitement.

Alexis cleared her throat and took a deep, quivering breath. "I thought you did just fine. It was a glorious day." Their eyes met again, and she told herself for the hundredth time that it hadn't been him. Having him look at her the way he did was proving to be the only bright light in her morning.

Nervously, Alexis awaited the opening of the bid. Harper had taken a seat next to Mr. Carson, but his eyes darted her way over and over again.

As she had in the past, Miss Sally seemed to be enjoying herself. She served fresh-baked croissants with melted butter, along with fresh-squeezed orange juice in small Waterford glasses. To Alexis it seemed as though there was only one person on edge in the room, and it was herself.

When they'd finished, Miss Sally slowly gathered up the dishes and took them into the kitchen, refusing all offers of help. Harper was commenting on the weather, but no one seemed to be paying much attention. Alexis was almost on the edge of her seat, nervously clasping her hands in her lap, awaiting the final outcome.

Carrying a round, silver tray in her hands, Miss Sally collected their bids. "Ladies first," she said after she'd sat down in a chair, a little removed from the others.

Alexis nervously picked at an imaginary thread on the cuff of her sleeve while she listened to the sound of the envelope being opened. When Miss Sally began to read the bid aloud, Alexis stared from face to face, seesawing back and forth between Harper and Mr. Carson.

Until Miss Sally had put down the piece of paper containing Alexis's bid, the pleasant expression on Harper's face never changed. When it finally did change, Alexis was thrown off-guard again. He looked over at her and winked, leaving her more perplexed than ever. Mr. Carson never took his eyes off Miss Sally's face, but his expression seemed a little too smug somehow. There was no way she could figure out what was happening.

Miss Sally plucked the next envelope up from the tray saying, "Mr. Carson's."

"Right," he smoothly agreed with a nod of his head.

Alexis thought she would never be able to sit still long enough to hear the bid. And when it came, she knew why. Five thousand dollars over hers, to the penny.

She'd lost!

Wanting to escape but knowing she couldn't, Alexis remained rooted to the spot, the hot, clammy feel of her hands turning instantly icy. She looked at Mr. Carson and saw him smiling at her. His smile said it all. He was the one.

She stared at him, wondering why she'd ever bothered to doubt that it could be anyone else. Briefly, she entertained the thought of telling everyone what had happened, but she remained silent. What good would it do?

"And last but certainly not least, we have Mr. Evans's bid." Miss Sally's hands fluttered to open the envelope.

They waited, and Alexis wondered what on earth the woman was reading that could be taking so long. She watched her read the bid over again, her brows furrowed into a confused frown.

"Mr. Evans, correct me if I'm wrong, because I'm a little unclear about this," Miss Sally stated. "Uh, the way I interpret what you have written is that the amount you are bidding is to be added to Miss Cartwright's bid and is to be considered a joint bid. Am I correct so far?" She peered over her half-moon reading glasses at Harper.

"Yes, that's absolutely correct." Harper looked directly at Alexis.

Alexis was dumbfounded. She was too full of conflicting emotions to make sense out of what was happening.

"Well, then, your bid added to Miss Cartwright's gives you two the new ownership of the Ebbtide Hotel. Congratulations to both of you." Miss Ferguson's voice was thick with pride.

"Now wait just a damned minute." Mr. Carson jumped up from the sofa. "I want to see that bid. Give it here." Grabbing it from Miss Sally's hands, he read both bids word for word.

"Again I have to say congratulations, my dear, and to you, Harper. I couldn't be happier." Miss Sally stepped over and shook hands with each of them.

It took all her inner strength, but Alexis stood up and leaned across the coffee table to receive the handshake. She didn't know what to think. The woman was saying that Alexis now owned the Ebbtide—just when she thought she'd lost it all. But it didn't make sense. How could she and Harper possibly share ownership? She couldn't believe her ears.

"I want to know just what's going on. There's nothing fair about this deal." Mr. Carson was fuming. His face had turned beet red, and he still had their bids clenched tightly in his outthrust fist. "I doubt if Miss Cartwright knows anything about this."

Alexis was in shock. Everything was happening too fast, but they were all looking at her, waiting for a response. It came automatically. "What makes you think so?"

"Well, I . . . well, you look surprised." Mr. Carson struggled with his words.

Alexis could feel anger quickly building up inside

her. Right now she hated Mr. Carson for his criminal behavior, and she hated the arrogant man who stood smiling happily over at her.

He'd made her love him, taken her on a spiraling ride to the heavens, and then assumed that because she'd committed that part of herself, she'd be willing to give up everything—her identity, her values, her very self. He hadn't even bothered to ask if she wanted a partnership.

What did it all mean? Why had he done it? Did he honestly believe that she was so shallow a woman that she'd sacrifice everything she believed in for his love? Did he expect her to help him destroy the Ebbtide?

Miss Sally poured champagne, and Harper passed around the glasses, oblivious to Carson as he angrily packed up his attaché case to leave. Harper handed Alexis a glass, ignoring the sad, shocked look on her face.

It was unbelievable. It had to be absurd. This entire thing was just a wild practical joke. None of it made any sense. In two flamboyant strides she was out of the room.

Harper watched her go, listening to the way her heels beat against the carpet. At least she hadn't refused. He breathed a sigh of relief.

Alexis was still too stunned to begin to make sense out of what had happened. Her head ached and her stomach was turning somersaults. Her arms and legs were weak and it was all because of Harper.

She couldn't believe, couldn't accept what his gesture had meant. How could he have so completely misunderstood her? She would never become a willing partner to the destruction of the Ebbtide, no matter what Harper wanted.

She knew if she could just manage to call up a sense of rage and indignation to mask her hurt she'd feel better, but right now shock wouldn't let her function. She hurried to the quiet safety of her room.

CHAPTER TEN

Harper pulled out his pocketknife and at the same time looked carefully down both sides of the hallway. Switching the roses from his right to his left hand, he stuck the blade of the knife into the door lock and twisted it until it finally gave. Then he stepped inside. His first thought was that she was gone. But her suitcase was on the bed, and he could hear a shower running in the bathroom. He reached back behind him and locked the door, latching the safety chain as an extra precaution.

He couldn't predict what she was going to do. When she'd left Miss Sally's apartment, he knew only one thing. He'd never seen a woman so angry. She'd misunderstood everything about the meeting, but he told himself he should have expected as much. One night together didn't mean smooth sailing forever. But what they'd shared meant he ought to try for it.

He opened the bathroom door and was met with a cloud of steamy vapor, along with a whiff of her intoxicating perfume. "Shame on you, Alexis. For a woman who thinks she knows so much about old hotels, you ought to know they make easy entry. Always lock and double-lock, even your bathroom door."

He walked directly to the tub and pulled back the curtain. The gasp of shock and the look on her face told him things might be even tougher than he'd thought. He stuck the roses between them. They'd be his first line of defense.

"What . . . Get out of here, you . . . oh, get out of here right now. How dare you!" she sputtered and raged. On the verge of panic, she brought her arm up, ready to swing at him. He'd antagonized her beyond the point of endurance.

He caught her arm on the downswing. "Wait, hold on!"

"No, you hold on." She tried to fight him.

"Here, choose a weapon." He offered her the roses, thrusting them at her so that she had to take them, and at the same time, he stepped into the tub with her.

There must have been two dozen of the salmon-colored rosebuds, and every one of them had thorns. She fumed, knowing she'd been tricked. With one hand she reached up and changed the direction of the nozzle.

Suddenly, Harper was sopping wet as he'd known he would be at some point. He felt the warm water hit him, and immediately resigned himself to the situation. His clothes would be ruined by the time he stepped out, but he didn't care.

"Proving a point to you is a very costly prospect," he said laughing, as water ran down his face in rivulets.

"Well, don't act like you're enjoying it so damned much. It's hard to work up much sympathy for a man who's grinning like a buffoon." She sighed and

180

pushed the roses back to him. "Get out, Harper. Now."

"Not until we've settled this thing." He let the roses fall to the bottom of the tub.

"Our lawyers can settle it. You'll be hearing from mine as soon as I get back to Houston."

As if just realizing she was naked, Alexis gazed down and hastily tried to cover herself. Her fury was tearing her apart, and she told herself the warmth and desire she could see in his eyes meant nothing to her.

"Get out, Harper, or I'll call security."

He laughed, that same, now familiar, rich, rumbly laugh of his. It hurt to hear it.

"Here, this is for you." Harper reached down to the tub bottom.

"What are you doing?" she screamed, and stepped back, jamming the faucets into her back. "Ouch."

"Would you just relax a minute?" He couldn't suppress a grin, holding up a thick brown envelope that had fallen with the roses.

They were a real pair. He watched her, thinking about the way she had reacted to him, first shock, then rage, then surprise, and then fear had registered in her eyes. The reaction he wanted to see was unlike any of those. Harper waited.

"Whatever it is, I'm not interested." She rubbed her back with one hand, holding the other across one exposed breast, twisting her body away from him.

"You ought to be. Inside is the title to the Ebb-tide." He leaned toward her. "That's what you wanted, isn't it?"

Gingerly, she moved back, aware of the metal faucets and how they could hurt, but even more aware of the effect Harper's presence was having on her. Her teeth began to chatter, whether from anger or fear or desire she wasn't certain.

"Alexis, I think you're right. And *we're* right, the right people to give the history of the Texas coast a boost."

She didn't know what he was saying. His dark eyelashes were matted together, and the water ran in steady lines down his face, cascading from his eyebrows onto his cheekbones and then along his lips. One stream of water ran along the curve of his jawline and off the tip of his chin. Alexis wanted to put her open mouth right on that spot and swallow the water from his damp flesh.

She knew that as long as she lived she'd never forget this sight of him—a vulnerable, powerful man. The thought of never being near him again was even worse than losing the Ebbtide.

"Please, Harper, get out," she begged, turning her eyes away from him.

"Not until we're finished with this," he answered.

She exploded then, like a volcano, catching them both by surprise. She pushed against his chest, wishing she were strong enough to shove him out of her sight.

"How," she cried, "how could you possibly assume that I would go along with your scheme? What did you hope to gain, Harper?" Her body shook with pent-up rage, and her voice quivered, as she stepped out of the tub, and grabbed a towel, wrapping it around her.

He opened his mouth, but she shook her head. She wasn't finished, not by a long shot.

"It's not bad enough that Mr. Carson or one of his hired burglars breaks into my hotel room and my attaché case, then makes his bid five thousand dollars more to the exact penny!" She was yelling now, but it made no difference. "Oh, no, that's not insult enough for me."

Adamantly, she shook her head from side to side. "Then you come charging in, and all of a sudden I hear you say in front of those people that you're placing your bid with mine!"

Her anger increased as she began to cry. "And that was the ultimate insult! For you to assume that because we'd shared some special moments out there on that sailboat, and because I had some very deep feelings for you, that I would give up everything I believe in and help you tear down this beautiful place . . . I-I think you're despicable."

Her cries had turned to sobs. "I'd never, never in a million years be that kind of woman."

He had listened patiently, hoping reason would prevail at some point. Standing beside her now, he looked at her imploringly. "I'd be that kind of man," he said simply.

"Ha."

"We'll get back to that point in a moment. Go ahead and finish." He wanted to take her into his arms and promise her everything would be all right. Her sobs were tearing him to pieces.

His calm levelheadedness made her cry even more. "Finish what? We are finished."

"No, I mean, tell me what else you thought."

"Okay, I will. All last night I wondered if you had been the one who'd broken into my room."

"You thought I'd been late to the dock yesterday because I'd been in your room?"

"You said you'd been studying."

He started to laugh then, a chuckle that was almost infectious. It made her stop crying.

"What's so damned funny?"

"I was studying all right. Do you want to hear about it?"

"No."

"I'll tell you, anyway. Did you know that this island was almost destroyed by a hurricane in 1900, and did you know that the Ebbtide remained standing with only water damage?" He watched her face, trying to gauge her reactions. "And did you know that we might be able to get State and Federal recognition if we're able to show that the restoration is totally in keeping with the period in which it was built?"

He'd studied hard the last two days, cramming in as much information as he could get his hands on. Before the day was over, he intended to explain how he'd developed such respect and admiration for her knowledge that he'd decided to follow her lead. Alexis knew what she was doing, he was certain.

Her mouth was slack with astonishment. She vaguely began to understand what he was talking about.

"Alexis, I wracked my brain, trying to think of some way I could give you a symbol of my love. I thought this was the way to show how much you and I needed one another." He gripped her arms with his

184

hands, forcing her to look at him. The touch of her skin was like a shot of adrenaline to him, and he kept talking.

"I was desperate, maybe too desperate, to be thinking clearly, but I'm in love with you. I'm desperately in love." He let go of one arm and brought his hand over to cup her chin, lifting her face toward his. "We're a team. We're not nearly as strong when we try to make it alone. That's what I wanted to prove. Maybe you didn't see my reasoning, but I think it's because you didn't trust me enough."

The tears started up again as she watched him reveal everything about himself to her. His voice rang with sincerity, and his eyes were full of loving compassion.

He saw her tears. "All right, I gambled, and I swear to God, Alexis, if you don't feel the same for me as I feel for you, then you can buy me out. One way or the other, the Ebbtide's going to be yours. That's all I wanted for you."

His face showed the pain and the fear of what she might say, but he had to risk his next statement. His entire future was riding on it, and he didn't know what else to do. "I want you to be my partner in business and my partner in life. That's all I want for myself, Alexis."

Alexis closed her eyes, hoping she wasn't dreaming. Filled with a warmth that knew no bounds, she was still afraid. "Are you telling me that you only wanted to make sure I got the Ebbtide? Or do you mean you've changed your mind and want to restore the Ebbtide?"

It sounded cold-blooded, she knew, but the issue of

the Ebbtide would tell her whether he really understood what Alexis Bain Cartwright was all about. Her heart stood still.

"There's one thing I'm going to insist upon. I've already talked to the historical society and a few local architects. I don't have all the details worked out quite yet, but there's a way to reinforce the foundation without disturbing the brick."

"Oh, Harper," she exclaimed as she reached out and pulled him to her, hugging him with a fierce surge of emotion. All the fear, all the anger left her without a trace.

"Grander than before," he whispered into her ear as he let himself respond to the intimacy of her caress. He didn't want to let her go. "I can see our advertisements now: 'A Texas showpiece, sparkling out of the shores of this great state like a diamond in the sky.' "

"There you go again," she said, pulling him closer to her.

"I love you, Alexis."

"I love you, Harper."

"You do?" It was the first time he'd heard those words from her lips.

"Yes, I do."

The sound of her words tore at his heart, and he wanted to shout his joy to the world. In a choked voice he said, "If what you're saying is true, how about us getting out of this bathroom now?"

They both laughed, and he kissed her, telling himself that the touch of her lips was a gift, a beautiful gift.

"Tell me again, tell me you love me," he breathed.

"I love you, Harper. I do." She clung to him, feeling his lips cover her with long, tender kisses, sliding his hands down to her waist and back. She'd never felt such love.

"We've got a lot to talk about, Alexis, like how this hotel is going to look and, most importantly, how soon you and I are going to be married. You will marry me, won't you?"

"Once we get out of this bathroom, yes." She laughed.

He laughed, too. "Look at me." His clothes were dark with water. His shirt clung to him like a second skin. His thoughts were on something else, however. "It'll have to be soon because we're not spending another night away from one another."

"Oh, Harper, how did we ever get off to such a bad start?"

"I don't know, Alexis. Each of us had a lot of things to resolve. Maybe this was the best way." He kissed the curve of her shoulder and then her ears and her nose, still marveling at the joy her words had brought him.

"I made a real mistake that first night with you, I was so self-absorbed." She wanted to explain, yet she knew there would be plenty of time. Besides, she was losing her train of thought with each press of his lips against her ready flesh.

"I want to hear all about it after you help me get out of these wet clothes. After we're married we're going to stay away from water for a while, okay? Maybe we'll honeymoon someplace where there's no beach, no showers, no water for miles around."

"Fine," she said, stripping away his heavy suit

jacket, letting it drop with a resounding splat into the bathtub. Next she attacked his shirt, calmly at first and then with steadily increasing impatience. The wet fabric tenaciously gripped the buttons.

"I'll be gentle with you," she teased, and then gritted her teeth and yanked at the offending cloth, tearing the buttons off all the way down.

Her rich laugh blended with his, and exuberantly their lips met in a kiss.

Alexis pushed the shirt back from his chest, then began to roll it off his shoulders. Her fingers were acutely sensitive as they explored his body. She kissed a mole she saw above his right nipple, then brushed her lips back and forth across the curly mass of hair on his chest. Aimlessly, she let her tongue wander across his flat nipples until she felt them become rigid.

Harper kept his eyes tightly shut, the better to concentrate on the sensual delight of her touch. Where their night together out on the sailboat had been a passionate coupling that knew no restraints, Harper intended for this time to be different. He covered her face with kisses, letting his hands run along her ribs and down to the narrow expanse of her waist as she drove him higher and higher with her roving lips.

He groaned with desire, and the low sound of his voice thrilled Alexis in a way she would be at a loss to explain.

Harper stepped out of his shoes and hastily pulled off the remainder of his soaking clothing.

"I was going to do that for you, Harper."

"I know, but another minute or two and . . ."

His firm, bold hands pulled the towel from her

body and scooped her up into his arms. He gripped her buttocks to him and carried her into the bedroom. She grabbed for a towel as they passed by.

"Wait," she said as he started to lower her on the bed. She partially covered him with the towel, rubbing the soft cloth against his buttocks and along his back in a gentle, slow pattern.

Harper's mind stopped working. He kissed her nose, her eyes, all the parts he had watched and wondered about in such mad confusion for so long.

Alexis wanted to—intended to—give herself wholeheartedly to him now. She knew that Harper felt the same, knew that he truly loved her as much as she loved him. Silently, she vowed she would be the woman he longed to trust.

Taking the towel away from Alexis, Harper dried her in lingering slow motion until he brought the towel up around her shoulders and pulled her to him. Picking her up, he lay her across the bed, watching how her skin turned a pale, pale peach as she got warmer.

In one fluid motion Harper gently took her in his arms. Her blood raced with anticipation, and she felt her skin glow with the warmth of her passion.

"You're magnificent," he whispered as he stared at her. "I'll never tire of looking at you."

Alexis smiled up at him. "Take all the time you want."

"I can't," he muttered harshly, his breath coming with difficulty. He bent his sleek head until his lips found a tender spot beneath her collarbone. Then they slowly moved up until he found her pulse spot, where he lingered. When he at last came to her lips, he crushed his mouth against them until he felt his teeth might bruise her soft flesh.

She was ready, thrilling to the pressure of his sensual, hard mouth. They had pledged their love and struggled to find this joy together. Now she wanted him to make ardent love to her, to appease her completely.

He eased his hungry body against hers, covering her slender frame with his. He brushed his fingers over her body until he found the damp, inner warmth between her thighs. Slowly, deliberately, he teased her to a shattering crescendo, their kiss deepening with each passing moment.

Her eyes were closed in the soft daylight, and she moved her head against the bed, feeling she might die from painful impatience or live forever, suspended in the exquisite pleasure of his intimate touch.

She caught her breath, wanting to cry out but desperate to hold on to the taut sensation that welled inside her. Finally, he lowered himself onto her, gathering her rich, ripe body to him.

Simultaneously, he leaned down to fiercely take her nipple into his mouth. He brought curved lips around the hard, brown flesh and drew in his breath. When he began to feel her body arch demandingly toward him, he gave himself up to the power of his desire. And then, with quick hot bursts of lightning, they rode together toward an explosive climax. The flame rocketed through each of them until they were one united spiraling arc of passion.

When the tremors had abated, they clung steadfastly to one another in the luxurious afterglow of their lovemaking. Alexis wondered if it could ever be like this again. Surely they had found the original secret—not everyone could know it.

After a while Harper began to kiss her swollen lips, and she felt her body responding, waking once more. She ran her fingers along his hips and buttocks, taking delight in the feel of his familiar body. Could they find that high, distant plane of consciousness again?

As her hands continued their intimate exploration, she heard a low, rumbling chuckle coming from Harper. Startled, she glanced up at him and found him grinning at her. "What's so funny?" she demanded.

"If you plan on continuing in the direction you've started, I think I'd better call room service fast," he replied.

Alexis stared at him, uncomprehending.

"For some oysters or Vitamin E or something," he said in mock desperation.

Her hands began to roam his body again, and her mouth toyed with the hair that fell above his ear.

"Never mind the order." He let out a deep sigh of contentment, full of joy and pleasure and love.

Alexis smiled softly to herself and continued with her quest, her heart filled with new meaning and purpose. She knew theirs was love in a special way—laughter's way.

Now you can reserve February's Candlelights before they're published!

- ♥ You'll have copies set aside for *you* the instant they come off press.
- ♥ You'll save yourself precious shopping time by arranging for *home delivery*.
- ♥ You'll feel proud and efficient about organizing a system that *guarantees* delivery.
- ♥ You'll avoid the disappointment of not finding *every* title you want and need.

ECSTASY SUPREMES $2.50 each

- ☐ 61 **FROM THIS DAY FORWARD**, Jackie Black 12740-8-27
- ☐ 62 **BOSS LADY**, Blair Cameron 10763-6-31
- ☐ 63 **CAUGHT IN THE MIDDLE**, Lily Dayton 11129-3-20
- ☐ 64 **BEHIND THE SCENES**, Josephine Charlton Hauber 10419-X-88

ECSTASY ROMANCES $1.95 each

- ☐ 306 **ANOTHER SUNNY DAY**, Kathy Clark..................10202-2-30
- ☐ 307 **OFF LIMITS**, Sheila Paulos 16568-7-27
- ☐ 308 **THRILL OF THE CHASE**, Donna Kimel Vitek.......18662-5-10
- ☐ 309 **DELICATE DIMENSIONS**, Dorothy Ann Bernard 11775-5-35
- ☐ 310 **HONEYMOON**, Anna Hudson...........................13772-1-18
- ☐ 311 **LOST LETTERS**, Carol Norris...............................14984-3-10
- ☐ 312 **APPLE OF MY EYE**, Carla Neggers 10283-9-24
- ☐ 313 **PRIDE AND JOY**, Cathie Linz 16935-6-23

 At your local bookstore or use this handy coupon for ordering:

Dell DELL READERS SERVICE – Dept. B503A
P.O. BOX 1000, PINE BROOK, N.J. 07058

Please send me the above title(s). I am enclosing $_____ (please add 75¢ per copy to cover postage and handling). Send check or money order—no cash or CODs. Please allow 3-4 weeks for shipment.
<u>CANADIAN ORDERS: please submit in U.S. dollars.</u>

Ms./Mrs./Mr._____

Address_____

City/State_____ Zip _____